the deadly conch
—tara trilogy—

Mahtab Narsimhan, a native of Mumbai, has always been fascinated by Indian mythology, fantasy and adventure. This came together with the unique cultural and spiritual energies of India in the critically acclaimed Tara Trilogy (*The Third Eye, The Silver Anklet, The Deadly Conch*), the first of which won the 2009 Silver Birch Award. She lives in Toronto with her husband, Rahul, and her son, Aftab.

the deadly conch

—tara trilogy—

mahtab narsimhan

RUPA

Copyright © Mahtab Narsimhan 2011

First published in India in 2012 by
Rupa Publications India Pvt. Ltd.
7/16, Ansari Road, Daryaganj,
New Delhi 110 002

Sales Centres:

Allahabad Bengaluru Chennai
Hyderabad Jaipur Kathmandu
Kolkata Mumbai

The Deadly Conch first published in English in 2011
by Dundurn Press Limited.

This edition published by arrangement
with the original publisher.

10 9 8 7 6 5 4 3 2 1

Mahtab Narsimhan asserts the moral right to be
identified as the author of this work.

This edition is for sale in India only.

Printed in India by
Manipal Technologies Limited
Press Corner, Manipal-576 104
Karnataka

For Rahul

one

Revenge

Layla glared at Tara, her face contorted with rage. Tara returned her gaze steadily. In the deepening dusk around them, the villagers of Morni danced in time to the drummer's beat.

For Tara, time slowed down, stopped, reversed. It was as if she were staring at a smaller replica of Kali; her evil stepmother, who had plunged to her death in the underground chasm mere days ago. Had it already been a week since she had escaped that nightmare? It seemed like yesterday.

Layla shall avenge my death … mine and Zarku's.

Kali's words, spat at her like a cobra's venom, still haunted her dreams. Tara sometimes awoke to the echoes of Kali's dying scream reverberating in her head. But did her spoilt, overweight daughter have the power to make them come true? Despite the heat, Tara shivered.

"TARA!" someone yelled.

She whirled around. Kabir, Raani, and Vayu raced up to her. Vayu limped slightly and Raani favoured one leg as she ran. Tara remembered their fight on the beach with the hyenas. Raani could barely walk then, a hyena had attacked Vayu as he struggled to keep their boat steady, and Kabir had been deep in the throes of fever. What a sorry sight they had all looked. But here they were now, alive and well! She had done the right thing by letting them escape, though at the time it had been a very difficult decision.

"You made it back!" said Raani. "I'm so proud of you." She flung her arms around Tara. Tara hugged her back, inhaling the intoxicating fragrance of the raat-ki-raani flower tucked behind Raani's ear.

Kabir and Vayu hugged her, too, grinning widely.

"You made it back with my sister and your brother!" said Kabir. "And you managed it all by yourself!" He shook his head, gazing at her, awestruck. "Weren't you scared? Did you ever feel you wouldn't be able to do it?"

"Our Tara is a tigress," said a familiar voice. "She prefers to work alone. *Nothing* scares her!"

"Ananth," said Kabir. "Good to see you, brother. That was some boat ride, no?"

"Hmmm, yes," said Ananth. "But it wasn't as exciting as the things Tara had to face."

Vayu clapped Ananth's back, smiling. And then they were all talking at the tops of their voices, bombarding

Tara with questions. Ananth had already told her how they had escaped, but their friends hadn't heard her story.

"I want to hear every little detail," said Raani. "Don't you dare leave out a single thing."

"Your leg," said Tara. "It's all right?"

Raani nodded. "Still hurts a little, but it's bearable."

"And you both?" said Tara, looking at Kabir and Vayu.

"We're fine," said Vayu. "But enough about us. How did you manage to kill Zarku *and* Kali? We heard so many different versions, but now you're going to tell us what really happened, right?"

"It's quite a story," said Ananth, smiling. But the smile did not reach his eyes. "It could take all night."

Something jabbed at Tara's heart. Ananth was mad at her for some reason. But why? Luckily no one else had noticed.

"Oh come on, Tara. Let's sit somewhere and talk," said Raani.

Tara led them to the periphery of the clearing. She glanced around, and, with a sharp jolt, realized that Layla had slipped away just when her friends had arrived. Layla's presence made her sick, but her absence made her worry even more.

"Ananth, did you see where Layla went?" asked Tara. "I should keep an eye on her."

"No, but don't keep our friends waiting. They're dying to hear your story. I must go see where Mother is." Ananth hurried off.

"Come back soon!" Tara called out behind him. Ananth disappeared into the crowd without looking back.

Men, women, and children thronged the clearing in their bright clothes and jewellery, shimmering and sparkling in the light of the torches that kept darkness at bay.

Tara paused for a moment, revelling in the festivities around her. All of Morni was rejoicing because of *her*. They could just as easily have been mourning the deaths of *three* children right now. She stood straight and tall, gazing at the smiling faces. She had believed in herself and it had worked. Though Tara prayed there wouldn't be another occasion for this kind of bravery, she knew now she could handle anything that came her way.

And yet, not everyone in Morni was happy tonight. They had lost Rohan to the hyenas. She could never forget him nor the look on his parents' faces when she had returned with Suraj and Sadia.

"Stop daydreaming and tell already," said Raani. "Don't keep us in suspense."

They all grabbed a cup of icy well water from one of the earthen pots placed all around. Then the four of them sat some distance away from the loud music and Tara began to talk. She told them everything. The journey back to the temple, finding Kabir's sister, Sadia, the trek to the underground cave, and the horror of discovering what Zarku had planned for her; cutting her heart out.

"So that voice you kept hearing," said Raani, wide-eyed. "That was Zarku's mother? You were possessed by his mother and you didn't know it?" She had twisted the edge of her dupatta around her fingertip, turning it white and bloodless.

Put like that, it sounded horrible. Tara suppressed a shudder. Reliving every moment of that ordeal, she couldn't imagine how she had survived. All alone.

The drummer picked up the pace of the pulsing music. Villagers dressed in clothes every colour of the rainbow, swirled and twirled in front of her, filling her field of vision.

Vayu shook his head. "You were incredible, Tara. To face Zarku in Kali's body and defeat both must have needed so much courage and a clear mind. I don't know if I could have thought of a plan, let alone carry it out."

"You think of nothing but food," said Raani. But this time there was no malice in her voice. Only laughter.

"But we all survived, thanks to Tara," said Kabir. "And Suraj and Sadia are safe, too. We did it!" He held out his fist just as he had the very first time. Smiling, Tara, Raani, and Vayu held out theirs, too. The fist was one again, except for Ananth. Why wasn't he back yet?

"The feast is ready!" a woman called out.

A last drum roll hung in the air for a few moments before evaporating in the thick heat of the evening. It was early summer and even the cloudless night was dressed in its best cloak, studded with stars. A full moon bathed the village with silvery light, making the evening appear magical.

Tara sniffed, her stomach growling. The fragrance of biryani filled the air, mingling with the delicate scent of chicken curry; her favourite. She had seen some of the village women prepare another favourite of hers: raita, the cool yoghurt sauce that she loved to drizzle over the biryani to cut the spicy taste. She couldn't wait to eat. And then sleep. It had been an exciting, but exhausting day.

"Everyone, gather around," said Raka. He clapped his hands and managed to get the attention of the villagers sitting in groups smoking, talking, and laughing. "I want to say a few words before we all start eating."

Everyone shuffled closer to Raka, who climbed on to the parapet surrounding the stump of the banyan tree. The sight of that burned stub jabbed at Tara's heart. Was it only last year that her grandfather, Prabala, had been tied to it while the villagers, changed into Vetalas by Zarku, had danced around the blazing tree, thirsting for his blood? She tried to block out the images of the transformed villagers with their translucent green bodies, pulsing black hearts, and turned feet. But Tara had defeated Zarku by turning his fiery gaze upon himself. They had all survived.

But not their poor banyan tree. It had taken hundreds of years to grow — and had been destroyed within an hour, thanks to Zarku. Tara missed its cool shade on a scorching summer afternoon, the swaying roots that hung from its branches, but most of all she missed the squirrels and birds that had made it their home and darted down fearlessly for tidbits offered by the villagers.

She missed Prabala, too. Shortly after she had returned with Suraj and Sadia, her grandfather had left for the hills to meditate. When Tara had asked why, he'd said that Morni needed stronger protection from the evils that had befallen it. The only way to achieve it was by more rigorous meditation on his part.

"But then who will look after us and heal us while you're away?" Tara had asked.

"The vaid, Vishnu, is my disciple and well qualified," her grandfather had replied.

"When will you be back?"

"When the time is right and no sooner." And then he was gone. No one knew when he would return.

When everyone had gathered, Raka began. "People of Morni, we are here today for two reasons. To rejoice because our very own Tara was able to rescue two of our children and stop ... Zarku ... from coming back." He hesitated, his face grim. Tara was sure he was thinking of the Vetalas. "But we are also here to remember Rohan, who is with us no more."

As he was speaking, Tara's parents, Parvati and Shiv, joined her. Tara glanced at her mother and smiled. Suraj scampered up and slipped his hand into Tara's. She had to blink back sudden tears as she realized, yet again, just how close she had come to losing her brother forever.

Raka finished speaking and loud applause broke out. He gestured to Tara, calling her over. Suraj poked her in the back when she did not move.

"Go on, Didi. You can't keep Rakaji waiting."

Tara looked over at Shiv and Parvati. Their faces were as huge and glowing as the full moon that hung low in the sky.

Parvati straightened the gold and green dupatta Tara wore, which matched her new shalwar-kameez specially stitched for the occasion. "You look beautiful, my star. Now go!"

Tara walked over to Raka and stood beside him, her cheeks burning. The applause was deafening. Raka held up a hand and the noise died down.

"Today we owe a huge debt to this brave girl who not only brought back her brother and Sadia, but rid us of Zarku. Because of Tara, every village for miles around respects Morni."

A sea of faces stared at Tara; some smiles were genuine, but some looked more like grimaces. She scanned the crowd and finally located the one face she had been searching for. Ananth stood at the back of the crowd. She smiled at him. An answering smile crept to his face.

He was so serious these days. She remembered the time when they were trying to escape Zarku and she had deliberately stayed on shore, allowing the others to escape. Ananth had looked so upset then and had been ready to jump into the water to rescue her but she had stopped him. He was such a wonderful brother to have, if only he'd remember to laugh once in a while.

"Who invited *her* to the feast?" a woman screeched. The anger in her voice was unmistakable. "Go away, you're ruining the celebrations!"

All heads turned toward the speaker at the back of the crowd. Tara saw a flash of white disappear into the shadows near the huts. It had to be Gayatri, Ananth's mother and a widow. None of the other widows dared show their faces at a public gathering but Gayatri-ma had always been different. Tara had forgotten how unwelcome widows were at any public gathering, joyous or otherwise.

"Gayatri," said Raka. "Come here."

There was no movement from the back of the crowd.

"Gayatri, don't keep me waiting."

Slowly Gayatri emerged from the shadows and walked toward Raka. The villagers hastily parted to let her pass. It was evident no one wanted to touch the widow or let her shadow fall upon them. They all believed it brought years of bad luck. Tara did not believe in such nonsense and therefore did not move an inch as Gayatri approached.

Gayatri stood in front of Raka with her head bowed, her saree covering her face, as was the custom. The villagers also considered it inauspicious to look upon the face of a widow, but Tara had no qualms. Gayatri-ma was like her second mother.

"Don't you know better than to come here today?" Rakaji's voice was calm, but tinged with annoyance. "Just because we allow you to live in the village does not mean that you break tradition and join in with the festivities. Remember your place and your duties as a widow. These rules were made for *your* well-being, as well as for the good of the villagers."

Tara's heart ached as she saw Ananth's mother shuffle uneasily in front of the gawping crowd, uttering not a word in protest. It was not Gayatri-ma's fault that she had lost her husband. Zarku was to blame! And just when she needed the support and companionship of the villagers the most, she was treated like an untouchable and denied the simple pleasures of life. It was so unfair!

"I really don't mind her being here, today, Rakaji," said Tara. "Gayatri-ma is like my own —"

"That's enough, Tara," interrupted Raka. His voice was as cold as the well water she had sipped moments ago. "No one asked your opinion about this. Do not interfere in custom and tradition that has been around long before you or I were born."

Tara hung her head and stared at the muddy ground that had been churned up by a million footprints.

"Sorry, Rakaji," said Gayatri softly. "Tara is like a daughter to me. I couldn't resist coming here to see her being honoured in front of the villagers. It will not happen again."

"If everyone starts forgetting their place, what hope is there for the rest of us?" said the crotchety old lady who had first noticed her. "Spoiled the entire evening by showing her cursed face. You mark my words; something bad is going to befall us all. Something terrible …"

"Shut up!" a voice yelled out.

Ananth stepped out of the crowd and stood by his mother, a ferocious scowl on his face. He had grown, and towered a good inch above Gayatri.

"You just leave my mother alone," he said looking around at everyone. "She said she was sorry. She only wanted to see Tara. If you don't want her here, then we'll both go." He glared at them all and then his eyes rested on Tara. He looked at her steadily, reproachfully, almost as if she were to blame for his mother's humiliation.

Tara tugged at Raka's hand. "Please, Rakaji. Just this once, let her stay."

Raka shook off Tara's hand with a disgusted expression and stepped away from her. "Rules are made for our good and *no one* can break them."

Not a soul piped in, but the unrest and animosity in the air was palpable. Tara looked at all of them, especially the women, decked in their fine clothes and jewels, proudly displaying the red sindoor, a sign that they were still married, in the parting of their hair. None of these women spoke up for Gayatri. Neither did her mother.

For the first time, it dawned on Tara that it was only that little bit of red powder that kept them on the respectable side of the fence. If they had the misfortune of losing their husbands, they would cross over to the "widow's side" and life as they knew it would end. The least they could do was love and support one of their own.

"Throw her out of the village," said a voice that made Tara's pulse race. "Just like you threw my mother out."

Layla pushed through the crowds and stood in front of Raka.

Tara's guts twisted into a painful knot. "Don't you dare compare Gayatri-ma to your evil mother, Layla," she said. "Your mother *deliberately* hurt others and *enjoyed* it. *She should never have been born.* I'm happy she's gone forever!"

Layla stared at her and Tara took a step back, shocked at the venom in the eyes of a child barely nine years old. Layla was the same age as Suraj and yet she looked years older. And capable of causing a lot of harm.

"That's enough, you two," said Gayatri in a surprisingly firm voice. "This is all because of me. I'm sorry to have spoiled your evening, Tara. I'll go."

"I'll go with you," said Ananth. He threw a last look at Tara and turned away. Tara's heart ached. Why was he angry with *her*? She'd tried to talk to Rakaji, but it hadn't worked. Did he not see that? She wanted to say something more, but the words had dried up under Ananth's angry gaze.

Once again, the crowd parted. Tara watched Ananth's stiff back and made up her mind to talk to him as soon as she could. She hated these silly traditions, too! Within seconds, Gayatri and Ananth melted away into the shadows beyond the circle of revellers.

Raka spoke again. "The food's getting cold. Let's eat and rejoice."

Instantly, Gayatri was forgotten as chatter and laughter swept through the crowds again. They all made their way toward the large, steaming pots of food prepared by the women of Morni. Banana leaves had been laid out on the ground in rows and the men and children sat cross-legged before each leaf-plate, waiting to be served.

Tara had been hungry earlier, but witnessing Gayatri-ma's humiliation had caused her to lose her appetite. Vayu, Kabir, and Raani were already sitting, awaiting their meal. Vayu's eyes were fixed on a woman coming down the line with a basket of pooris.

"Aren't you joining us, Tara?" asked Raani. She patted a spot beside her. "We have to eat and then head back home. We'll have to start out as soon as possible."

Tara shook her head. "You all eat, I'll be back soon with Ananth."

Tara hurried down the line toward the woman with the pooris.

"Want one, Tara?" said the woman. "They're hot and fresh."

Up close, the fragrance of the fried bread tickled her nose and her stomach growled again.

"Yes, please," said Tara.

The woman picked out the biggest golden orb and handed it to her. Tara thanked her and hurried on, munching on the poori while searching for Ananth.

Something warm brushed against Tara's leg. A stray dog was looking up at her, his enormous eyes riveted to the food in her hand. He whined and wagged his stump of a tail.

"I'm hungry, too," said Tara taking another large bite of the fried bread. "You'll just have to wait till the feast is over. I'm sure there'll be lots of leftovers. You'll eat like a king tonight."

"Oi, Tara," a women called out. "Don't feed that stray. They're getting to be too much of a nuisance."

Tara looked down at the dog again. His tail fanned the air vigorously and his eyes pleaded silently. She backed away. He limped toward her, uttering small pitiful squeaks. Large patches of brown fur were missing and the outline of his ribs was clearly visible, like a serrated bowl covered with skin. Tara couldn't resist him anymore. She broke the poori in half and held it out. The dog lunged forward and snatched the food from her hand, his teeth grazing her knuckles.

"Owww," she said, glaring at the stray and rubbing her hand. "You sure have that pitiful performance down pat until you get the food!"

In reply, the dog jumped again, surprisingly high, and snatched the other half from Tara's hand and swallowed it.

"You mangy thief!" Tara swiped at the dog, but it backed away.

She heard laughter from a few onlookers who had witnessed the scene.

"Told you not to feed him," the woman said before moving away. "Rakaji is going to have all the strays rounded up and put to sleep. They're hungry and getting very aggressive. He's afraid they might bite a child."

Tara looked at the dog, who now sat licking his injured paw, the food long gone. She was mad at him. But it was not his fault that he did not have a loving home. Putting the strays to sleep would be a mean thing to do. Killing anything, for that matter, would be wrong. How could you take something that you were unable to return? *Especially a life.*

But you've taken two lives, said a small voice within her. *You killed Zarku and Kali.*

That was different, she told herself. They were inhuman monsters. The last few moments in the cave flashed through her mind once again; Kali's screams as she had hurtled to her death. She clapped her hands over her ears. Would she ever be able to forget? Would time ever dim this ghastly image? Everyone thought she was a hero; they envied her, but they had no idea about the terrible nightmares she had. The memories she had to struggle hard to forget, lest they overwhelm her.

"You're happy that my mother is dead," a voice whispered in her ear. "Isn't that what you said?"

Tara's skin crawled. She did not even have to turn around; she knew who it was. A voice that oozed such hatred could only belong to one person. She stood still for a moment, wishing Layla would go away.

Layla grabbed Tara's shoulder and spun her around. Her black eyes glittered as she held Tara's gaze. "Watch your back, *dear sister*. I'll make sure you suffer horribly for what you did to my mother. That's a promise."

two

The Temple is Defiled

Tara was trapped!

Kali blocked one side and Zarku, the other. Both were aflame. Arms outstretched, they advanced slowly and deliberately. It was utterly dark in the forest and the only light came from their blazing bodies. Tara whirled around, tensing for the sprint to safety. Too late. Layla stood right behind her. She seemed even more massive than usual, moving with surprising speed. The trio moved in on her, closer and closer. Heat fanned her face; the smell of searing flesh poisoned the air. Kali reached out, her burning fingertips inches away from Tara's face. Any moment she'd go up in flames, too.

"I'll make you suffer," hissed Layla. "You. Will. Suffer." And then she enveloped Tara in a bear hug.

Tara screamed. She sat up on her cot, soaked in sweat, the thin sheet wrapped around her body like a python.

23

The courtyard was silent except for the pounding of her heart. Above her, stars twinkled weakly in the fading night. Suraj lay on his own cot, undisturbed by Tara's yell.

Tara heard the echo of her scream, very faint this time. Had someone really screamed, or was the sound inside her head? She hugged her trembling body, breathing deeply.

"Tara, what's the matter?" Parvati stood framed in the doorway, a lantern in hand. "Are you all right?"

"I-I … uh … had a bad dream," said Tara finally. She could barely think of the words let alone speak.

"Do you want to sleep inside?"

"No, Mother. It's too hot. I'll stay out here."

"All right," said Parvati. She came over and kissed Tara's forehead. "You're safe now. You have nothing to worry about." Parvati adjusted the sheet over Suraj. With one last look at Tara she went back inside.

Tara lay back and gazed at the sky. She breathed in the night air tinged with heat and the earthy smell of manure from Bela's stall. She was at home with family! She had nothing to worry about except Layla. Tara repeated this over and over again, but it gave no comfort at all.

Her mind returned to her dream and she shuddered. Not one, but *three* of the most evil people she had ever known were haunting her. But two of them were gone forever. Or were they? She pushed the thought out of her head and focused on something else that nagged at her. The second scream? Now that she thought about it, she was sure it wasn't in her head. Who had it been?

"Psssst." The sound came from behind the low wall which circled their courtyard at the back of the house.

Tara sat up, straining to see who it was. A snake? An intruder? Layla? Her heart slammed against her ribcage.

"Psssssssssssssst." She heard it again. More insistent this time. And then someone whispered. "Tara, it's me."

Gayatri-ma! Tara jumped off the cot and raced barefoot to the edge of the courtyard. She opened the rickety wooden door as quietly as she could and peered out.

There stood Gayatri, a ghostly apparition in her white saree. Her eyes had a hunted look. In one hand she clutched a pooja-thali. The other fluttered at her throat like a trapped bird.

"Is everything all right?" asked Tara. "Ananth? Is he —"

"You have to come with me, now!" Gayatri-ma's voice trembled. "Quick, wear your mojris and follow me."

Tara raced back to the cot. She slipped her feet into the mojris, taking care to shake them out first. Scorpions, spiders, even tiny snakes were known to crawl into shoes during the night and bite the toes of a person foolish enough to slip her foot inside before checking.

Tara's head whirled with a million questions, making her dizzy. Whatever it was, it must be serious. The usually serene Gayatri was definitely rattled. But what or who could have scared her so much?

Tara looked around for the gold and green dupatta she had curled up with that night, but it was nowhere to be seen. She was tempted to run inside the house and get another. Leaving without it made her feel as if she was half-clad.

"Hurry, Tara!" whispered Gayatri-ma from the doorway. "Before the sun rises and the rest of the villagers awake. *We have to go now.*"

Tara heard the deadly fear in Gayatri-ma's voice and decided to skip the dupatta. Hopefully she'd be back before any of the village gossips awoke and accused her of running around improperly attired. Now that she was thirteen she was considered to be a young woman and expected to act her age and dress accordingly.

"Where are we going?" said Tara. Gayatri had set off down the road at a fast clip, darting fearful looks around her. It was just before dawn and no one was about.

"Ganesh temple," said Gayatri. A hare streaked past them suddenly and they both stopped in the middle of the road, watching it go. A faint breeze lifted the edge of the saree that always covered Gayatri-ma's face and the full moon shone on it. Tara gaped at her. She looked so young, so beautiful. Somehow, it seemed like she was looking at Ananth's mother for the first time. In spite of the urgency of the moment, Tara couldn't help the sadness that filled her at the thought of Gayatri-ma's joyless existence.

"Did you go to the Ganesh Temple last night?" said Gayatri suddenly.

Tara jerked out of her reverie. "No."

"Are you sure? You better tell me the truth!"

"I *am* telling the truth!" said Tara. "I had no reason to go anywhere. I was so tired, I didn't even change before falling asleep. I woke up screaming because of a bad dream and then I think … I think I heard another scream. But I'm sure I must have imagined it."

Gayatri swallowed and shook her head. "That was me. And we're very, very lucky that no one else heard the scream. We better hurry. There's something you need to see."

They hurried in silence toward the Ganesh Temple. Around them, the sky was turning into slab of pale pink shot through with ribbons of darkness. Birds chirped overhead, their piping and trilling growing stronger by the minute. Gayatri hurried on, panting for breath, and Tara followed, her stomach queasy.

The temple steps came into view.

"Come on," said Gayatri. "There's no time to lose."

They ran up the steps. Gayatri-ma had to stop and hold a stitch in her side, but she wouldn't let Tara go on ahead. Tara's curiosity was a large balloon inside her, threatening to explode. What was it that Gayatri-ma had seen early in the morning? And why was she taking a risk by hanging around? Widows were supposed to complete their visit to the temple and go back home before anyone else woke up. The villagers considered it very unlucky to see a widow first thing in the morning.

They reached the doors of the temple, gasping for breath. Tara had always loved coming here. Often, she would sit at the feet of Lord Ganesh and pray. And it was here that she had first met Mushika, the Lord's companion, when she had rescued him from the cat. This was always a happy place for her and instantly she felt a little calmer. Nothing bad could happen in the house of God.

"Come on, Gayatri-ma. Tell me what's happened," said Tara. "Surely it can't be that bad?"

"Go inside and see for yourself." Gayatri's face was very pale. She was watching Tara the way a hawk watches its dinner.

Tara stepped inside the small room. The oil lamps that normally burned at the feet of the deity had gone out. The room was quite dark.

The first thing that hit her was the smell. It reminded her of the underground cave, of Kali and Zarku. It was so overpowering that Tara's stomach heaved.

It was the smell of death.

It took a moment for her eyes to adjust to the dimness. There was something on the floor that shouldn't have been there. A shadowy lump and a splash of colour. Bright red. Tara stared at it, uncomprehending.

A rosy finger of dawn light stole in through a window and pointed to the floor, illuminating the scene.

Tara clapped her hands to her mouth as bile shot up her throat. She shuddered, tears pricking the backs of her eyes. Her stomach was a tight knot. She had to get out, get out *now*! She couldn't bear to look at it anymore.

Tara whirled around and found her way barred. Gayatri stood there, her face whiter than her saree. "So you didn't do this?" she asked.

Tara shook her head. If she opened her mouth she knew she'd vomit.

"Tara, you can tell *me* the truth," said Gayatri softly. "Whatever it is, I am here to help you. Ananth and I owe you a debt. If it hadn't been for you and your family, neither of us would be alive today. You've been under a lot of pressure, lately, so I can understand if ..."

Tara pushed Gayatri aside and stepped over the threshold, gulping in the clean air. Her nausea subsided temporarily, only to be replaced by a throbbing anger.

"How can you even say that, Gayatri-ma? Do you really think ... I'm capable of ... that?" The world spun around her and she held her head in her hands until it subsided.

"Look again and you'll see why I'm asking you this question. Why I brought you here."

'I can't go back in there," said Tara. "Please don't make me."

"Tara, you have to. Take a proper look, but hurry. Punditji will be here soon to prepare for the day's pooja. We have to clear this mess before someone finds it."

Tara balled her hands into fists, took a deep breath, and went back inside. There on the floor lay the stray dog she had fed the previous evening. Someone had hacked his neck and it was almost severed from his body. It lay in a pool of blood, thick and viscous. Flies buzzed over the body greedily. The dog's eyes were open. He stared straight at Tara accusingly.

Tears dripped down her face. Who could have done something this terrible? In a temple? Automatically she reached for the edge of her dupatta to wipe her eyes. Her fingers closed on thin air and she remembered she wasn't wearing one. She wiped her face on her sleeve instead.

"It's over there," said Gayatri, still watching Tara. "But you'll never be able to use it again."

"What?" said Tara. She wiped another tear on her sleeve.

"Your dupatta," said Gayatri. She pointed at the dead animal.

Tara noticed it then. Her gold and green dupatta was pinned under the dog's body and soaked in blood.

"Now you know why I came to get you?" said Gayatri softly. "This is what you were wearing yesterday, isn't it?"

All the words inside Tara dried up. She pushed past the older woman, raced outside once again and retched. How had her dupatta gotten *here*? And what would happen if someone found it? She stopped mid-retch, ice creeping through her veins in spite of the warmth that held the promise of another hot day. The sun had already started to paint the bottom of the temple steps in gold.

"I didn't do it!" said Tara. "You have to believe me."

"I do," said Gayatri. "But will anyone else? Your dupatta is proof that you were somehow involved."

"But I just saved the villagers from Zarku. They believe I'm a hero. And everyone knows I hate killing anything. How could I do something like this in my own temple? No, we'll just go and tell them it has to be someone else. No one could believe I did this."

"Tara, long ago I realized that superstition and fear are stronger than reason, stronger than anything else. If Punditji finds this inside his temple, it will not take him long to condemn you, too. You'll go from hero to zero in seconds."

Tara looked into Gayatri-ma's eyes, which held a world of truth and pain. Here was a living example of how blind superstition could be. Tara didn't stand a chance.

"Then we have to get rid of it!" said Tara, unable to suppress the panic in her voice. "Now. Please help me, Gayatri-ma."

"Why do you think I came to get you?"

"We need a sack or something to put the body in," said Tara. "And my dupatta. I don't think I can bear to look at it ever again."

"I'll go get one," said Gayatri. "You try and pull the body to the back of the temple so at least no one will see it when they walk in. We also have to clean up the … mess. Hurry!"

Tara looked fearfully behind the deity at the door that led to Punditji's quarters. He would be arriving any moment now to wash the fruits and flowers for the pooja. He would distribute these to the villagers who would pass through the doors all day.

She strained her ears, but there was no sound of movement. Maybe he, too, had slept in after last night's revelries. Thank God for that. The next moment she shook her head. A horrible thing had happened in God's house and she was *thanking him* that she had not been discovered.

Gayatri ran off to get a sack and Tara stooped over the body, staring at it, trying not to gag and cry at the same time. As the light grew brighter, every detail became clearer. The wound in the dog's neck was deep; he had been attacked with a curved sickle the farmers used to cut grain. Who could have been heartless enough to take a weapon to a helpless animal? Her legs turned rubbery and she reached out for the wall to steady herself.

There lay her dupatta, wedged under its body, the blood making the green appear darker. Her eyes strayed to Lord Ganesh. *Why Lord*, she asked silently. *Why did this happen? How can you allow an innocent animal to be murdered within your home?*

Her mother's words came to her, as they always did when she was troubled. *Things always happen for the best. Sometimes, when they occur, you will probably be very unhappy, but as time passes, you will see that the pattern makes sense. It always does.*

Yet Tara could not believe that this death and her dupatta being there made any sense. Someone was trying to frame her! And if it was discovered, she would be in deep trouble. She had to hide the dog. She stepped closer to the body. The whiff of decay and blood was overwhelming. The cloud of flies was getting thicker. She touched the dog's hind leg. It was cold and stiff. She jerked her hand away, her insides burning and cold at the same time. How was she going to do this?

The temple bell at the top of the steps pealed loudly. Tara jumped. They had left it until too late. Someone was about to enter, and, as was customary, he or she had rung the bell. Tara raced to the body and slipped in the pool of blood. Down she went, cracking her knee on the stone floor. Biting her lip to stop the howl of pain she tried to pull her dupatta out from under the dog. It was glued to him. Tara took a deep breath and scooped the body up in her arms, dupatta and all, trying not to faint as the smell hit her like a slap on the face.

Just as she stood up, Raka's wife, Sumathy, stepped into the temple with her thali. Her eyes travelled from Tara's face to the bloody, dripping bundle in her arms, to the pool of deep red on the floor.

For a moment the only sound in the temple was the buzzing of the flies, indignant about their meal being snatched away.

The next moment, Sumathy screamed and collapsed on to the floor in a dead faint.

— three —

The Nightmare Begins ...

"**I** didn't do it!" said Tara. "You have to believe me!" Sweat beaded her forehead and heat prickled her back as if a million tiny red ants were swarming all over it.

Tara stood beside the burned stub of the banyan tree where the Panchayat and villagers had gathered. Some gaped at her incredulously, others shook their heads and clucked their tongues. Children craned their necks to get a better look. Once again she was the centre of attention. But this time she wasn't enjoying it one little bit.

This time, when Sumathy had screamed, Punditji had come rushing out of his room. One look at the dead animal in her hands and he had howled in anger, rousing the entire village. Even though the dog was long buried, its stench, the slickness of its blood on her hands, its eyes staring at her unblinkingly, was indelibly printed in her mind. She wouldn't forget this incident for as long as she lived.

"But Tara," said Raka, "how can you explain your dupatta near that dog? Everyone saw you wearing it at the celebration last evening. And then it was next to the dead dog. How did that happen?"

Tara shook her head. "I can't explain it. When I fell asleep, the dupatta was with me. This morning it was gone."

Raka narrowed his eyes. "If you say you didn't do it then how can you explain that it was *you* who found the dog first thing in the morning?" he asked. "That you were obviously trying to hide it when my wife caught you." His eyes pierced her, and for a moment Tara was afraid that his shrewd gaze could see right into her soul. "Are you in the habit of going to the Ganesh Temple first thing every morning?"

Tara's heart twinged as if a hand were squeezing it. She knew he would ask this question and she had struggled with the answer; the only one that would spare Gayatri-ma. Should she mention that it was the widow who had woken her and brought her to the temple? She knew what Raka's next question would be; if Gayatri-ma had seen this defilement of their temple, why hadn't she woken Punditji instead? Why Tara?

The people of Morni barely tolerated widows, and to bring one more thing to bear against Ananth's mother would make them despise her even more. It was a good thing that Gayatri-ma had not been around and Raka's wife had only seen her.

"Speak up, Tara," said Raka. "You have nothing to worry about if you tell us the truth."

Tara's heart was racing; her mind was in a whirl. Easy for him to say, sitting up on that platform, looking smug. Much as she respected Raka, he had no idea what a widow had to live through, day after tedious day. No man in the village could ever imagine it. Nor a woman, until she was in the same situation.

"Tara is innocent!" said Parvati. Her voice quivered with emotion. "Tell them, Shiv. It's ridiculous even to have this meeting. She must have panicked seeing her dupatta there and acted without thinking. That's all. But she did not do this."

"Yes, Raka —" Shiv started to say.

"I'd rather you didn't interfere," said Raka, cutting him off. "I think Tara is old enough to think and speak for herself."

Ignoring him, a few villagers piped in.

"How can you accuse Tara of something like this?"

"She's our hero! She saved us from Zarku."

"There has to be another explanation."

And then there were the ones who were clearly jealous of her. Their accusations flew at her like poison-tipped arrows.

"I think she did it. She has become too arrogant ever since she came back with the children."

"Maybe some of Zarku's madness rubbed off on her."

"Do you think she's still possessed by his evil mother, Zara?"

Tara was aghast at the last question. "NO!" she said. "That's not true. Zara is dead and gone, and so is Zarku. I'm innocent."

The hot sun burned Tara's scalp and yet her hands were cold and clammy. If the villagers started believing *she* was possessed, she was in for a very rough time. Their blind superstitions would make her life a living hell. She had to stop them thinking this way!

"THAT'S ENOUGH!" said Raka. "This is not a free-for-all. The Panchayat will investigate this incident thoroughly. And since it was Tara's dupatta which was found there, we shall start with her. No one but Tara is to speak."

This time no one said a word except for the black crow perched on the stump behind the Panchayat. It cawed raucously, then flew off.

Tara opened her mouth. *Tell the truth*, the small voice nagged at her. *One lie will lead to another and then another. You'll get stuck in a web of lies. Tell the truth.*

Gayatri-ma's face flashed in her mind. The look on her face when Rakaji had ordered her to go home the day before still made Tara burn with shame. No, she couldn't involve Gayatri-ma. She would have to take the blame and hope that as time passed, the villagers would forget about the incident.

"I had a very bad dream last night," said Tara. "I woke up screaming. Ask Mother, she heard me."

All faces turned to Parvati, who sat in the front row, clutching Shiv's hand. Her mother nodded as soon as Raka glanced at her. "It's true. Tara decided to sleep in the courtyard with Suraj since it was too hot inside the house. Early this morning I heard a scream and ran outside. Tara was awake and shaking. I asked her to come inside, but she refused. She said she was all right so I left her and went back to sleep. I assumed that Tara had dozed off, too." Parvati's voice was tinged with fear and Tara hated herself for putting her mother through this.

"Then what happened?" asked Varun, a member of the Panchayat.

This is it, thought Tara. *Either I tell the truth now or never.* Her eyes flicked over to Ananth at the periphery of the crowd. He looked grim. How much did he know? Had his mother confided in him? If she told the truth, would the villagers allow Gayatri-ma to stay in the village? And if she was forced to leave, Ananth would leave, too! She would lose her brother and a woman who was a second mother to her, all at once.

"What's taking so long, Tara?"

"She's making up a good story," said a child's voice.

Tara started. There was Layla in the front row. Somehow she hadn't even noticed her. The nightmare flashed through her mind and Tara hugged herself to stop from shuddering. She would not give this fat lump of a stepsister the satisfaction of seeing how rattled she was.

Layla's black eyes were riveted to Tara's. She could almost detect a hint of glee in them. Up until now her only two pastimes were eating and sleeping. Evidently she had a new pastime: torturing Tara.

"Shut up!" said Tara. "I'm not like you or your miserable mother. Lying is in *your* blood, not mine. Thank God one of you will never trouble us again."

"How dare you insult my mother," said Layla. "You're the liar and I'll make sure the villagers know it."

Tara's skin prickled again as she remembered Kali's last words. What if they weren't an empty threat? What if this was the first step to avenging her death? Tara clenched her hands and shoved them into her pockets. It was too much to think about at the moment.

"Stop it," said Raka firmly. He glared at Layla first and then at Tara. "This is not about Kali or how you two feel about each other. All we need to know is why our temple was desecrated, and more important — *who* did it?"

"There is another matter, Raka," said Varun. "Punditji has been ill since last night's feast. That's why he awoke late and the temple was unattended all of last night and this morning. It's possible that he ate something bad, but now I wonder ..."

"Varunji," Layla piped in, cutting him off. "We all ate the same food. Yet no one else is ill. It's possible that something was deliberately slipped into Punditji's food."

Loud gasps peppered the air. Tara's heart skipped a beat. Put that way, she was under more suspicion than ever! And Layla was making things worse. She had to clear her name before it was too late.

"We're still waiting, Tara," said Raka. "Now's your chance to speak. You won't get another."

Tara took a deep breath. "I was scared, Rakaji, and too restless to go back to sleep. So I decided to take Mother's advice and visit the Ganesh temple to calm my mind and give thanks for our safe return to Morni."

Out of the corner of her eye she saw many villagers nodding their approval. So far, so good.

"Last night I was too tired to change so I went to bed in the same clothes I had worn to the feast. I had my dupatta with me when I fell asleep, but when I looked for it in the morning, it wasn't there. I thought Mother might have taken it inside so I didn't give it another thought. Someone could easily have taken it in the middle of the night and put it next to the body. In fact I'm sure that's what happened. You must believe me."

"Liar," said Layla.

"Shut up," snapped Tara. "No one asked you to butt in."

"Layla, you will keep your opinions to yourself until Tara has finished," said Raka. "One more word out of you and I'll have you thrown out immediately."

Layla muttered under her breath, glaring at Raka and then at Tara.

"Continue," said Raka. His face was very troubled.

The sun climbed higher in the vast blue sky. There was not a cloud in sight and no shade either. The tense silence in the clearing made even the drone of an inquisitive bee seem deafening. Tara had a pounding headache. Would they believe her? There was only one way to find out.

"So I went to the temple," said Tara. "It was very early in the morning and I saw no one."

"Not even Gayatri or any of the other widows?" asked another Panchayat member. "Surely someone must have seen you?"

Tara blanched and hated herself for that instant reaction. "No," she said. Her voice shook. She cleared her throat. "Sorry," she whispered, licking her lips. "I'm so thirsty. But no, I didn't meet anyone. I reached the temple, saw the dog lying there and I … I …"

"Realized that while you were defiling the temple and insulting Lord Ganesh in a bout of complete madness, your dupatta had fallen off. So you decided to retrieve it and that's when you got caught," finished Karthik, a dour-faced member of the Panchayat. The contempt in his voice cut Tara to the core. "Do you have any idea what you've done, Tara? This could easily bring the wrath of the gods upon our heads. We will have to pray very hard to beg for forgiveness and I hope it's not too late."

An agitated hum rose from the crowd.

"That's not what happened," said Tara turning to the villagers. "Why won't you all believe me?"

"She's right," said Parvati, getting to her feet. "I know my Tara. She would never kill a fly. It is unthinkable that she would hurt an innocent animal, let alone kill it so mercilessly. There has to be another explanation. And Layla, if you say one more word against your sister, you're in deep trouble!" Her mother glared at Layla, who met her eyes without flinching.

"Let's all calm down for a moment," said Raka. He wiped his face with the end of the red turban and looked at the other members of the Panchayat, a perplexed expression on his face. The others looked equally grim and confused. Raka beckoned and they gathered closer, talking in low whispers while Layla chattered to the villagers sitting next to her.

Tara rubbed her sweaty palms against her kurta. What if they found her guilty? Would they turn her out of Morni, too? Where would she go? Around her, the crowd's whispers grew louder, angrier. The more she thought about it, the more certain she was that Layla had something to do with this. But could she have thought of this all by herself? No, it was impossible. Someone more devious had thought of this simple way to frame her.

Kali. Just thinking of her brought goosebumps to Tara's arms. That could be the answer. Somehow mother and daughter were still connected and she had to break this connection between them before it was too late.

"Is there anything else you want to say, Tara?" said Raka. "Say it now before we announce our decision." Tara could not make out the look in his eyes, but his voice was heavy with disappointment.

Tara stood tall. She was innocent and she was not going to cower with guilt. "Members of the Panchayat and People of Morni. I love this village. It is my home. I have put my life in danger to keep it safe. I was the one who faced Zarku, not once, but twice. I rescued my brother and brought him back, alone. You cannot truly believe that I would do something like this. Someone else killed the dog and made it look like I did. I have been framed. You can choose to believe it or not, but I did not do this."

Tara walked on rubbery legs to the front row and collapsed next to her parents and Suraj. Her heart raced and her mouth was dry. The Panchayat stood up this time and moved away from the crowd as they held a hurried discussion.

"Didi, I believe you," said Suraj. "Here's my favourite marble. You can have it. It'll make you feel better."

Tara took the marble and slipped it into her pocket, trying to smile. Her mouth refused to co-operate. Suraj clasped her hand tight and Tara squeezed her eyes shut to stop the tears that were threatening to spill over. Raani, Vayu, and Kabir had left right after the feast, so she had no one she could discuss this with. Ananth was sitting too far away, though she had hoped he'd come over to talk to her. Together they would figure out who was responsible. She had to talk to him as soon as this was over.

"The Panchayat has made a decision," said Karthik. "Raka will announce it."

There was an immediate hush. Tara's heartbeat slowed. Every throb was loud in her ears. What had they decided? She couldn't wait to find out and yet a part of her didn't want to hear it.

"Everything that Tara has accomplished for Morni has been taken into consideration," said Raka. "While this horrible incident is still a mystery, it cannot be denied that Tara's dupatta was found there. We will investigate this matter further, but we're all shocked that someone in this village was cruel enough to kill a helpless animal in such an inhuman way. Though all the evidence points to Tara, it seems unlikely she could have done this. I personally believe she was framed."

Raka looked straight at Tara and she gave him a small smile. He nodded imperceptibly as his eyes swept the rest of the crowd.

"Rakaji, you should start the investigation with Layla," said Tara. His belief in her innocence had emboldened her.

"Let me finish," said Raka. His voice was hard. "I hate interruptions and accusing anyone without proof is wrong! The Panchayat will report back to all of you as soon as we've found anything."

Tara looked at the ground, burning up with shame. It was because of Layla that she was facing this humiliation. Layla had it coming to her, she would see to it.

"In the meantime, Tara, you will wash the temple inside and out thoroughly, no matter how long it takes. Then you will help Punditji keep it clean for one more week. Is that understood?"

Tara nodded as the uproar behind her steadily grew stronger.

"Is it wise to let the person who defiled the temple back near it?" someone said.

"Have her clean up the whole village not just the temple," a woman called out.

"This is an unfair punishment for a child. Tara didn't do it," said Poonam, their neighbour, who was very fond of her and Suraj.

Tara pulled at a stray weed poking up from the parched earth. Her blood boiled and not because of the midday sun. Some of the villagers speaking against her were the same people she had risked her life for; people she had saved from spending the rest of their lives as Vetalas. And yet, based on this one incident, they were ready to condemn her. Tara felt a hand on her shoulder. She looked up.

"It's all right," said Parvati. "We'll get to the bottom of this. If Father were here, it would have been very different, but we'll have to manage on our own until he returns."

"Serving God is a good thing and Lord Ganesh knows you didn't do it," said Shiv. "Even if he cannot give evidence on your behalf."

Tara nodded, grateful for their support. Even Suraj flung his arms around her and squeezed her tight.

"The meeting is over," said Raka. "You can all go back to work."

Tara started walking, scanning the crowd for Ananth, but there was no sign of him. He must have slipped off to tell his mother the news. At least she had managed to keep Gayatri out of this. It was the only thing that gave her some solace.

"Suffer!" A sibilant whisper close to her ear made her jump.

Tara turned around. Layla stood there, sneering at her. Tara felt a deep pang of fear. For the first time in her life she saw purpose in Layla's eyes — other than the desire to stuff her face full of food.

Tara then knew with absolute certainly that Layla was behind this. But how was she going to prove it to the villagers before it was too late?

— four —

A Deadly Rumour

Tara had never worked so hard in her life, not even when Kali had been around, treating her and Suraj like slaves. She worked from sunrise to sunset, scrubbing, scouring, and washing. Tara spent extra time on the spot where the blood had pooled and seeped into the floor, trying to remove every trace of that terrible incident.

All prayers had stopped while she cleaned the temple. Tara had to endure the malevolent looks of Punditji, who had recovered sufficiently from his illness to supervise her every minute of the day when he wasn't sleeping or eating. It was like a vacation for him and he was enjoying it tremendously, but tried hard not to let it show.

Punditji also delighted in sneaking up on her, barefoot, and yelling in her ear. After the fifth time, Tara took to looking behind her every few minutes to see if she could catch him in the act.

"You missed a patch there," he said one hot afternoon. "If you work this way, it'll never get done."

"I just did that section," she replied. "Look, it's still wet."

Tara tried hard to keep the disgust out of her voice. He looked like an overgrown child who had not done an ounce of work in his life. His soft, white hands had only ever held pooja thalis laden with fruits, and the prayer bell. Once he blessed the food it was divided equally between the devotee and God. And God really meant Punditji. No doubt, missing all those treats was making him cranky and he blamed Tara for it. This was his way of making her suffer as much as him.

"Are you implying that I'm a liar when the *real* liar is you?"

Tara opened her mouth, and then closed it again. With a sigh, she pushed the bucket over to the section Punditji had pointed out with his big toe, and started scrubbing. It was the third day of her punishment and she was still working on the inside. She hadn't even begun to clean up the outside. Punditji had made her start with his living quarters at the back of the temple. It was not part of the punishment, but Tara did it, anyway, trying not to show shock at the mess.

The bell outside the temple pealed loudly, shattering the heavy stillness of the afternoon. They both looked up. Raka stood there, wiping his perspiring face and fanning it with the edge of his turban. He stepped inside and touched his forehead to the Lord's feet. Then he turned to them. "How is the cleaning coming along?"

Tara wasn't sure whom he was addressing so she kept her mouth shut and continued scrubbing.

"Slow. This one is very lazy," said Punditji. "But don't you worry, Raka, I'm keeping a close eye on her. She will not get away with a shoddy job. Once she has finished the outside of the temple, I will bathe Lord Ganesh in milk. Then we will organize a grand pooja for the entire village."

Hmmm," said Raka. "How long will it take?"

Punditji stroked his ample belly and tugged on the little shendi of hair at the back of his head. "A week at most," he said.

A week! thought Tara. Her arms were threatening to fall off within the next hour.

Raka sighed deeply, staring out the doorway. "We also have to do a pooja for the rains. The monsoon season has started and yet, not a drop has fallen from the sky. Our crops are starting to turn yellow and the well water is running low. We need rain *now!*"

"At this time last year, the crop was bountiful and green," said Punditji. "This year the gods are angry with us. Can you blame them, with sinful children like Tara in the village? They're punishing us, that's for sure. But do not worry, Raka. I have just the prayer for it. It's expensive, but it'll be worth it."

Tara sat back on her haunches, her heart beating erratically. Now they were blaming *her* for the delayed monsoon? Were they mad?

"We've had rains fail before so I don't think we can put *all* the blame on Tara," said Raka. But he did not sound very convincing, almost as if he had trouble believing his own words.

Tara's eyes met Raka's, but there was no warmth in them. No smile on his face, either. He had been so happy when she had returned with Suraj and Sadia. He had embraced her warmly and said that she had upheld the name of Morni. It hurt more than anything to see distrust and doubt where once there had been pride and joy.

"But yes, there is a possibility that the gods are angry with us," said Raka. "Last week the clouds had started to gather and this week, nothing but blue skies."

Tara resumed scrubbing, her chest burning with anger. They were wrong. All of them! She had to prove it. But how?

"I have to go," said Raka. "Let me know the moment this is done. We have much to pray for!"

Once again, he supplicated himself in front of Lord Ganesh, then left without glancing at Tara.

The moment Raka was out the door, Punditji said, "I have some important work to take care of. See that you don't disturb me for the next couple of hours. And when this room is done, you can start on the steps." And with that, he shuffled away, barely able to suppress a yawn.

Tara stood up and stretched her aching back. She walked to the doorway and stared at the flight of steps. She had run up them so often, never giving a thought to how many there were. She counted them for the first time. Thirty-one long slabs of stone that she had to scrub and wash. She lifted her eyes to the huts that spread out before her, to the paddy fields beyond, which were yellow rather than the lush green she loved to see. It stabbed at her heart. Among these were her father's fields, too. The sky was still blue and cloudless. Did the rain have to be delayed just now?

"Oi!" said Punditji. "You can admire the view later. Get to work."

Tara jumped, a curse at the tip of her tongue. He had done it again. She felt an irresistible urge to empty the bucket of dirty, soapy water over his spotless white dhoti and then see him yell. But she was in enough trouble already, so she resisted the impulse and got to work until the vast, glowering bulk of Punditji moved away. The door to his room slammed shut. At least she would have peace for a couple of hours while he took care of *important matters*, his afternoon siesta. Everyone knew about it, but no one dared say a word for fear of his wrath.

She paused to brush her damp hair from her eyes and gazed at the figure of Lord Ganesh. The brilliant sunshine that poured in from the windows and doorway made the colours seem even more vibrant. The gold ornaments adorning his body glittered, throwing bright, starry reflections on the ceiling. She looked into the eyes of the clay deity. They were so skillfully painted that no matter where she stood in the room, it seemed that Lord Ganesh was looking straight at her.

"Why," whispered Tara. "What is this pattern you're weaving for me now which I can't see? And what is it going to look like when you're done?"

The Lord continued looking at her serenely, and, in spite of everything, Tara felt a calm descend upon her.

"Talking to yourself, Tara?" said a sneering voice. "You better get used to it because soon no one in Morni will be speaking to you."

The calm evaporated as Tara turned around. Layla filled the doorway.

"Get out," said Tara. "I'm working."

"Didn't look like it a moment ago," said Layla. She stepped into the temple and deliberately walked over the damp patch that Tara had just cleaned, leaving large, muddy footprints. She walked over to the spot where the dead dog had lain. "So this is where you killed it, right?"

Tara stood up, her heart pounding. She had scrubbed the spot over and over until there was no telltale sign of blood to mark the place. Yet Layla had known exactly where it had been.

"It was there," said Tara. She pointed to a corner of the room while watching Layla carefully.

"Wrong!" said Layla. "It was right he —" She stopped.

52

"So it was *you* who did it," said Tara softly. She came right up to Layla and stared into her black eyes. "You did it and framed me."

"Prove it," said Layla. She stared right back at Tara without the slightest hint of fear.

A tidal wave of rage almost drowned Tara, but she knew she couldn't do anything for now. She was dying to push Layla out the door and see her bump down each one of those thirty-one steps. Instead, she shoved her wet hands into her pockets. In one of them was a smooth orb.

"I can't prove it just yet," said Tara. "But you won't get away with it. I'll see to it that everyone knows."

Layla giggled and at that moment it seemed as if a shrunken Kali had returned from the Underworld. She scooped up a spotted apple still lying in one of the thalis and bit into it. Tara dropped to her knees and surreptitiously pressed her wet palm into the vermillion powder that the villagers sprinkled on the Lord's feet as part of their offering.

"I've got something for you," said Tara. She slipped her hand back into her pocket. "Here — it's the dog's eyeball."

Layla stared at the dark, black orb smeared in red that lay in Tara's bloody palm. She gave a loud shriek, dropped the apple and raced out the door, retching.

"Come back, you forgot your souvenir," said Tara trying not to burst into laughter. She watched Layla stumble down the steps, almost tripping over her own large feet. Tara silently thanked Suraj for his favourite marble, making a mental note to return it to him soon.

That felt good.

Tara washed the vermillion powder from her hands and started scrubbing once again.

• • •

The Ganesh temple thronged with villagers and the overflow spilled out on to the steps and around the sides. They were here for the grand pooja that Punditji had organized for the village of Morni. Every man, woman, and child was decked out for the occasion in spite of the searing heat of the late evening. The men wore white kurta-pajamas that were already limp from the humidity, and the women were in sarees or ghaghra-cholis. Gold ornaments shimmered on them, catching the dying rays of the sun.

Tara gazed around with pride. The temple sparkled. The stairs leading up to the deity room, all thirty-one of them, were clean and free from years of accumulated dust and dirt. The floor of the main room was pristine. She had scrubbed away all the layers of spilled diya oil, sticky fruit juice, coconut water, and ash from the incense sticks. The black stone slabs shone and were smooth against the soles of her feet. The thick, heavy fragrance of sandalwood incense perfumed the air.

Tara had even pulled out all the weeds around the periphery of the temple. She had replaced them with small, flowering plants that had flourished in the hot sun, their orange and red hues contrasting with the grey stone of the temple walls.

"This room smells so good and it's spotless," Parvati whispered to Tara as they stood in a corner. "I never could stomach the odour of rancid oil for long. You've done a very good job. I'm sure Lord Ganesh is pleased with you."

"Thank you, Mother," said Tara. "Maybe Lord Ganesh is pleased, but Punditji still isn't."

Mother shook her head and hugged Tara. "Don't mind him."

"Mother, did Rakaji ever find out who killed … who did this?"

Parvati shook her head. "They are still investigating, but *I* know you didn't do it. Your father believes you're innocent, too."

Tara noted that very few villagers were of the same mind as her mother. They stopped to talk to Shiv and Parvati, and patted Tara on the head. Most just nodded in Tara's direction and faced the deity, waiting for the pooja to begin.

You're all wrong, thought Tara. *And when the truth comes out, you'll see.*

The small room was hot, made hotter by the rows of diyas lit at the foot of Lord Ganesh. Everyone wanted to be inside rather than outside, and the crush of bodies was almost unbearable. Many fanned themselves with their turbans or sarees, their faces glistening with sweat. Tara couldn't wait to get out and breathe the cool air, but she would not miss this for anything. She had been ordered to clean the temple and she had done a great job. And she wanted to see the Panchayat's reaction to it.

Punditji stepped out from his room in a crisp white dhoti. "All ready?" he boomed. His chest was bare except for the thick, red thread that circled it diagonally, from over his right shoulder to his ample waist. It was part of a coming-of-age religious ceremony that all Hindu boys went through. His curly pigtail was well oiled. Suraj had once remarked that it looked like a pig's tail. Ever since, Tara had to suppress a smile whenever she gazed at Punditji's shendi. His small eyes glittered as he saw the piles of fruits and sweets on the glistening steel thalis at the foot of the deity. Nothing put him in a better mood than the sight of food. And today it was evident that he was in an excellent mood.

Raka and the rest of the Panchayat were the last ones to arrive. A place next to the deity had already been reserved for them. As soon as they took their places, the pooja began.

Punditji tinkled the bell and led the villagers through a prayer they could sing, all together. The chants of the villagers echoed in the small room. Tara gazed at the face of Lord Ganesh, thankful that things were back to normal. After this, the villagers would forget this incident had ever happened and no one would look at her like she was a pariah.

Once they finished chanting the prayer, everyone fell silent. Punditji then sang the next prayer solo. His nasal, whiny voice mingling with the heat and smoke from the incense sticks made Tara drowsy.

Sumathy stood beside Raka. She had barely spoken to Tara since that incident. Tara caught her eye and smiled tentatively. Sumathy looked away and it felt like someone had slapped her. Tara scanned the crowd and one by one, the villagers' gazes slid away. She had completed her punishment. Why were they still angry with her?

She looked around for Ananth, but didn't see him. Maybe he was outside with his mother. If Gayatri was attending, it would be best to remain out of sight.

With a pang of worry, Tara realized Layla wasn't there, either. Her drowsiness vanished. *Where was her stepsister? What was she up to now?*

"Mother, where's Layla?" whispered Tara. She remembered the look on Layla's face when she had held out the marble, pretending that it was the dead dog's eyeball. Her stepsister was not likely to forget that joke.

"I don't know," said Parvati softly.

Tara nudged Suraj, whose eyes were closing as he stared at Punditji's back. "Suraj, have you seen Layla?"

"Obviously, some people think that the pooja is not important enough to pray in silence," snapped Punditji. He twisted around, his eyes fixed on Tara. "Silence," he hissed.

Burning with shame, Tara stared at Punditji and then at the rest of the villagers who wore expressions of annoyance and disgust. "Sorry," she whispered.

Punditji threw her one last dirty look and resumed the prayers. Seated on a flat, low stool, he held the little bell in his left hand. It tinkled nonstop while he threw flowers and rice at regular intervals at the foot of Lord Ganesh. The incantations got louder as Punditji exercised his considerable lung power in front of a captive audience.

One thought continued to nag at Tara: where was Layla? It was not like her to avoid a large gathering if she could help it. She got the answer a second later.

"Rakaji, RAKAJI!" someone yelled outside the temple.

Tara knew that voice. Hated that voice. Yet she couldn't wait to hear what it had to say.

Punditji huffed loudly, barely able to twist around on his stool without falling off. "What is it with these interruptions? Is anyone going to let me finish this pooja? The auspicious time is ticking away."

No one answered him. Their eyes were glued to the door as the crowd parted. Layla stepped through the doors, gasping and wheezing for breath, her large hand clasped to her pudgy chest. It was as if someone had lifted Tara from summer and thrown her straight into winter. Cold seeped through her as she watched Layla doing a great imitation of a fish out of water.

"What is it, Layla?" said Raka when Layla showed no signs of stopping her infernal panting. "How dare you interrupt this important pooja? Couldn't you have waited?"

Layla stopped immediately. She pushed past villagers and came closer to Raka. She folded her hands and bowed her head to Lord Ganesh before speaking.

"Rakaji, this was something that just couldn't wait. In fact, we may need Punditji's prayers more than ever now, or we are all doomed."

"What are you talking about?" said Raka. "Speak clearly, Layla or get out. You're trying my patience!"

Layla glanced over at Tara for a mere second, but it was clear there was more trouble coming her way. Tara clasped her hands together, not surprised to find that they were sweaty.

To fight Kali and Zarku, who were openly evil, was one thing. But to fight a child, merely nine years old, was another. Who would believe that Layla was plotting to make her suffer? No one would believe that this spawn of Kali was more dangerous than her mother, simply because no one would ever suspect that a child could be this devious. She was more formidable an enemy than her mother or even Zarku.

"There's a dead cat in our well," said Layla. "The water is undrinkable."

The villagers gasped collectively.

"What?" said Raka. "How can you say that?"

"Because I was with Sushila Mausi just now, drawing water from the well. The bucket was so heavy that the poor lady could not pull it up by herself. So I stayed to help. And when the bucket came up ..." Layla paused, her eyes sweeping the room. Only when she was satisfied that all eyes were upon her did she continue.

"There was a dead cat in it," she whispered. "And cats don't jump into wells for the fun of it."

"This is very serious," said Raka. "Already the water level is low and now if the water is contaminated and there's no rain ..." His eyes flicked to Tara.

"I didn't do it!" screamed Tara. "She's lying."

The villagers jumped and so did Punditji, upsetting a diya in front of him. All eyes were on Tara and she had to fight the urge to run and hide from those accusing glares. "I was here all the time, Rakaji, just as you had instructed. Ask Punditji if you don't believe me," said Tara. She scrubbed her sweaty palms on her kurta again and again.

Punditji reluctantly nodded.

"I never said you did it," said Layla. She looked calmly at Tara. "Why would you think that?"

Tara's guts twisted into knots as she realized what she had done. She had walked right into that one, with her eyes wide open. For a mere child Layla was very smart. Too smart. With a thrill of horror, Tara realized that if Layla could manage this level of deception at such a young age, she would get worse with each passing year. They were nurturing another Kali. Morni was truly doomed. And so was she.

"I-I thought you ..." muttered Tara and stopped. The disapproving looks around her had dried up the words.

"Rakaji, the village of Chandi Mandir also shares the water from our well," said Layla. "They'll have to be told right away."

Raka looked as if he was in pain. In fact, all the members of the Panchayat looked troubled.

"This is not good," said Sumathy. "First the dog in the temple, now the cat in the well. What is happening to Morni?"

"Bad luck, Sumathyji," said Layla promptly. "That is what's happening to Morni. And there is only one person here who has spent time with the most evil person of all — Zarku. And she's brought that evil to us." She raised her chubby finger and pointed. "Tara is to blame for this."

Her words, mingling with the sandalwood incense, sped through the room and beyond. Then the whispers started.

It's Tara ... she spent time with the evil Zarku.
Tara brought bad luck to us.
Tara is bad luck.

five

The Hidden Snake!

A million eyes pinned Tara where she stood. The room was hot, but now it seemed as if she were standing in the heart of a volcano. Sweat oozed out of every pore and her clothes stuck to her like a wet sheath. She tried to meet everyone's gaze defiantly. *You're wrong*, she wanted to scream at them. *Dead wrong*. But their disapproval and anger were too much to bear. She dropped her gaze, an icy panic flooding her. She had saved her brother, Sadia, even her friends from a horrible death. She had faced Zarku and Kali alone, not wishing to put anyone else in danger. But Layla had twisted this around to make it look like she was tainted. As if *she* were the evil threatening Morni.

And the villagers were starting to listen to her!

"The pooja —" Punditji started to say.

"You've all gone mad," said Shiv, cutting him short. He gripped Tara's shoulders and glared at the villagers.

She was thankful for his support because her legs were so wobbly; it took all of her willpower to keep standing.

"You're accusing my daughter for bringing bad luck to our village just because Layla, *Kali's daughter*, suggested it? Have you forgotten what Kali was like? *She* was the one who invited Zarku to the village. She and her corrupt father, Dushta. If it hadn't been for her, my daughter wouldn't have had to put her life in danger; not once, but twice! You should be ashamed of yourselves. All of you!"

The villagers shifted uneasily and looked away. No one uttered a word.

"You have a point, Shiv," said Raka, breaking the ominous silence. "Morni has had its share of good and bad luck over the years. I have seen it all; failed crops, drought, illnesses, malaria, and famine. But never," he said, glancing at the Panchayat, "during my time as Head, has our temple ever been defiled by a dead animal, nor our well water contaminated. Am I right, brothers?"

The others nodded, still staring at Tara.

"Can we finish the pooja?" whined Punditji. "These interruptions are one too many and I don't like it."

"With all due respect, Punditji," snapped Parvati. "This is more important." She addressed Raka in a shrill voice, the light of battle shining in her eyes. "And you think my daughter is responsible for these incidents? The heat has softened your brains, Raka."

"There is no need to be rude, Parvati," said Raka. "I want to get to the bottom of this, too. But you have

63

to admit that the timing could not have been worse. We need the rains and there is none. We need the blessings of the Lord and the temple was defiled. We need water desperately, and now our well is out of commission. All of this happened within a week of Tara returning." His voice had sunk to a whisper as he said the last few words. His normally soft eyes were like black stones.

Tara moved closer to Parvati and clutched her hand tightly, hoping she would wake up soon and find herself back in bed. This nightmare was even worse than the one she'd had earlier in the day.

"You're wrong!" said Suraj suddenly. "My Didi would never harm anyone. I'll fight anyone who says so."

Tara tousled his hair. "I'm all right, Suraj, but thanks."

"I think we should all calm down and finish the pooja," said Karthik. "We can finish this discussion later."

"Oh no, take as much time as you need," said Punditji. "I can't finish the pooja now." It was evident from his sulky expression that he was unhappy about the spotlight being snatched away from him once too often. "The auspicious time has passed. We'll have to do it some other time. Go home, all of you."

For a moment there was complete silence and then everyone spoke at once.

"No, we want prasad," yelled the villagers. "We need the blessings of Lord Ganesh. Finish the pooja."

"No," said Punditji. His bald head shone with sweat and his pudgy arms were crossed over his hairy chest.

"You can take all of your offerings away. They have been partially blessed. That's the best I can do right now."

A buzz ran through the crowd. Never before had Punditji stopped a pooja in the middle. This was another first and Tara could sense their resentment turning to shock and then to anger. It came hurtling toward her in a huge, towering wave and crashed down.

"Punditji, for all our sakes, could you please complete the pooja?" asked Raka.

Punditji drew himself up. "No! The favourable time is past and I will not do it today. You may take your duties lightly, Raka, but I do not."

It was Raka's turn to look sulky, but he did not say a word. Tara looked from the chief to Punditji, her heart unbearably heavy. She had imagined month-long festivities upon her return; being honoured and treated like a queen. The reality could not have been further from her dreams. Her eyes came to rest on the person who had started this.

Layla stood next to Sumathy, trying to act calm, but her eyes gave her away and Tara knew she was very happy. Raka tried to quiet the crowd and send them home. Slowly, the temple began to empty. Punditji was talking to the Panchayat, gesticulating in agitation. Tara strained her ears, but she could not hear a word of the whispered conversation.

"This is really bad, Shiv," said Parvati. "What's happening ... and why? We have to talk to Layla tonight. By attacking Tara in public she's causing a lot of tension and fuelling their superstitions. This is so wrong."

"We told you she was evil, Mother," said Suraj. His eyes shone with anger as he thumped his small fist into his palm. "Tara and I had warned you, but you wouldn't listen."

Tara, Shiv, and Parvati gaped at him.

"What did you say?" said Parvati.

"When Kali was thrown out of the village, you offered to look after Layla, remember?" said Suraj. "We knew she was just like her mother. She always tried very hard to get us into trouble. It made her happy to see us sad. She's doing it again."

Parvati drew in a shaky breath, but did not reply. Tara could only think of the ruined evening. Surely this was one more black mark against her. The last of the villagers were streaming out. The Panchayat and Punditji were still talking in whispers, glancing their way now and then. Layla seemed glued to Sumathy as they stood a short distance away from Raka.

Shiv herded them together. "Let's go home. We need to have a serious talk."

Parvati called out to Layla. "Come on, Layla. We're all going home."

Layla stared at them, blank-faced, as if strangers had asked her to accompany them home. "I'm staying here," she said. "I have to talk to Rakaji as soon as he's free.

There are a few more things I have to tell him." She stared straight at Tara.

Tara had to use all her discipline to hold Layla's gaze without shuddering or glancing away. *This is a child, a mere child*, Tara told herself over and over again. *And you can beat her. Be strong.*

"You snake," hissed Parvati. "I brought you up like my own daughter instead of an orphan. And this is how you repay me?"

"I have done nothing," said Layla.

Her parents looked at each other and then back at her.

"You can stand there and say that?" said Parvati in a choked voice. "You're feeding the villagers lies about my Tara and turning them against her. She is your sister, after all. How can you do that to your own family?"

"*Stepsister*," said Layla. "You may have taken me into your house, *Parvati*, but you never took me into your heart. I don't think I'll call you Mother anymore."

Parvati gasped. "You ungrateful ... lying ... little —"

"I think you better go, Parvati," said Sumathy. "Harassing a child is the last thing I'd expect from you. Especially a child who has no parents to protect her." She put an arm around Layla who moved closer, a terrified expression on her face.

"We are — were — her parents before she decided to start playing these games," said Parvati. "Since Kali left, I have brought her up as one of my own. I have no idea why she is telling these lies all of a sudden."

"Let's go," said Shiv, his voice grim. "I think we've heard enough. Layla, we need to have a talk, all of us. Either you come with us now, or you never come back."

There was silence in the room. Tara realized that Raka and the rest of the Panchayat were suddenly standing beside them. Punditji had disappeared into his room.

"Are you threatening a child?" asked Raka. "You, Shiv? Don't you know better?"

"Raka, this is not what it looks like," said Shiv. "I want to get a few things straight, as a family, and up until this moment I thought Layla was part of it."

There was a huge sob. They all looked at Layla. "I don't want to go with them," she wailed in pitiful voice. Her tears came thick and fast. "They'll punish me, for sure. Maybe even beat me up for saying bad things about their *real* daughter."

Tara felt increasingly numb. There was a part of her that was horrified and yet she couldn't help marvel at the way Layla was manipulating the situation. Her stepsister had always been able to turn on the tears at will. Those tears had earned her many beatings from Kali.

"Don't be silly, Layla," snapped Parvati. "We've never raised a hand to you. Ever!"

Layla ignored her. She slipped her hand into Sumathy's. "Please let me stay with you for a few days. I'm scared to go back with them."

Sumathy looked at Raka. He looked at Tara, then at the rest of her family. He wiped his face and nodded.

"Only for a few days. Until ... until we sort all this out. I can't take every child into my house, but this is so unusual ... all right." He sighed deeply. "I still have to talk to the headman of Chandi Mandir about the well. We'll all have to find another source of water."

The mention of water made Tara realize that she was parched and they could not draw water from their own well. They would now have to walk a few kilometres to the village of Pinjaur to get the water, and haul it back, pot by pot. It was going to be very hard and the villagers were going to hate her more than ever.

• • •

"Shiv, you have to knock some sense into Layla," said Parvati. "This is going from bad to worse." She took a sip of the hot ginger tea Tara had made for all of them.

Tara slumped against the wall of their tiny kitchen. Night trickled in through the bars of the window set high up in the wall, adding to the gloom. She sipped her own tea, feeling a river of warmth slide down her throat and heat up her icy insides. The little food she'd just eaten sat in her stomach like boulders.

"How can I argue with a child?" said Shiv. "Besides, the villagers are already starting to believe her. She's played the right card by preying on the villagers' superstitions."

"I can go and beat her up!" said Suraj. "I never liked her, anyway."

In spite of the worry ballooning inside her, Tara had to smile. Suraj looked so indignant as he waved his fist in the air. So different from the woebegone boy she had rescued from the cave. Involuntarily, she glanced at his forehead. It remained unblemished and flat.

"I will, if you want me to, Didi," said Suraj. "And after that, Mother, you can punish me for beating up a girl. I won't mind."

"Suraj, I don't want any talk of violence in this house," said Shiv. "We've seen enough of that when Zarku was around. If you must beat someone, do it with your head, not your hands."

"There is one person whom the villagers will listen to," said Parvati. Her eyes sparkled in the orange glow of the kitchen fire. "Prabala."

A little firework of joy exploded in Tara's heart. Of course! Why hadn't she thought of it before? "Where did he go, Mother, and when is he coming back?" asked Tara.

Parvati sighed. "That's the problem. When Father goes off for meditation, he very rarely gives an exact location. He said he was going to the Bhakti Ashram in the Himalayas. As for coming back, it could be days, months … even years."

The firework fizzled out. Tara clasped the hot cup of tea tighter, but it was no match for the deep chill spreading inside her.

"Then I'll go looking for Prabala," said Shiv. "We

need him here, with us. Once the Panchayat of Chandi Mandir hears about the contaminated well, things could get ugly for all of us. Especially with Layla continuing to spread lies about our Tara. That's what she's probably doing this very minute."

"She said she was going to make me suffer," said Tara suddenly. She had not confided in her parents earlier, not wanting to worry them, but now she couldn't keep this to herself any longer.

In the dying embers, she saw the enlarged whites of their eyes, their grim expressions as they stared at her, aghast.

"Is she going to kill you, Didi?" asked Suraj. His face crumpled.

"Not if I can help it," said Tara. With a huge effort, she smiled and ruffled his hair. "Hey, don't you have any faith in your sister? I defeated Zarku. Layla is a little chicken in comparison. If I wanted to, I could fix her like that!" Tara snapped her fingers. The click was loud in the quiet kitchen. They heard the faint tinkle of Bela's bell as she moved around restlessly.

Suraj hugged Tara tight. "I wish Layla would go away and never come back," he said.

"Let's all sleep on it and talk in the morning with a clearer mind," said Shiv. "Tara, from now on I want you indoors at night no matter how hot it is."

Tara nodded, not really paying attention. An idea was pushing up through her mind like a magic weed, growing taller and stronger by the second. She couldn't wait to put it into action.

• • •

As Tara sat up slowly, the cot creaked. She froze, an excuse ready at her lips. But no one stirred.

Watery moonlight spotted the floor. Tara watched the silver discs appear and disappear as clouds moved past the face of the moon. She was reminded of the night, a little more than a year ago, when she had seen the black cobra— her mother in disguise — come up to them. How scared she had been when the snake had kissed Suraj first and then her. And now she was scared again. Of a child this time! She shook her head; she had braved worse dangers than a spoiled, vindictive girl. She would get the better of Layla. And Ananth was going to help her. He would know what to do.

She tiptoed to the kitchen, turned around at the threshold, and looked back at the sleeping faces of her family. After such a long time they were together again, and they deserved some peace and happiness. She was going to see to it that they did.

Tara slipped her feet into her mojris, unhooked the metal clasp securing the back door, and ran out into the warm night, praying that her plan would work.

six

Whispers in the Night

Darkness shrouded Ananth's home. It was long past midnight and he was sure to be asleep. Tara tiptoed up to the mud hut and peered in through the nearest window. Darkness peered back at her. But she knew their home so well, that even without any light she knew how the cots were positioned and where Ananth would be sleeping.

The cloudy night did not make things easier. Tara waited, trying not to drum her fingers on the windowsill, until the moon wrestled free from the clutches of the dark clouds and showed its face again. Its weak light illuminated the inside of the hut and her breath caught in her throat. Ananth's cot was empty. His mother was fast asleep.

Where was Ananth and what was he doing out of bed this late at night?

Tara sank to the ground, her mind whirling like a leaf in a hurricane. Ananth had barely talked to her these last few days. She missed his teasing, his smile, but especially his protectiveness toward her ever since she had braved many dangers to bring him back to life.

She remembered their escape from the forest when she had tricked them all into going off without her. Had there been fear on Ananth's face or annoyance as the boat shot away? And the evening of the feast when she had recounted her adventure for her friends, he had been absent.

A thought struck her — was he really busy or was he avoiding her? Now that she had thought about it, she had to get to the truth. Immediately. She couldn't live for one more moment with this on her conscience.

Tara stood up and wiped her damp forehead with her palm. Her kurta was plastered to her back and she reeked of sweat. If only it would rain! So many clouds in the sky, but not a single one lingered. They all rushed past, probably to another village that was worthier of their life-giving water. Was Morni really going through a bad time because of her?

Stop being silly, said the small voice within her. *Go talk to Ananth. That's why you're out here, anyway, right?* She had come to trust that voice now. And that was exactly what she was going to do. But where was Ananth? In the kitchen getting a drink of water? Out with friends? There was only one way to find out.

Tara kept to the deep shadows as she padded toward the back of the hut. Nothing stirred, no one spoke. More clouds sailed overhead, devouring the patches of moonlight on the ground. The darkness intensified momentarily.

Tara rounded the side of the hut and heard whispers. She stopped immediately and dropped to her knees, listening hard. A boy and girl were talking.

"It's late and you should not be here," he said softly.

That was definitely Ananth. Tara leaned closer. Whom was he talking to in the middle of the night? A secret love? The thought almost made her giggle out loud as she tried to imagine Ananth with a girlfriend. What a time she would have teasing him about it tomorrow.

"I thought you should know," said the girl. "You're her brother."

Tara clamped her hand over her mouth to suppress the involuntary gasp. The world spun around her. She squeezed her eyes shut, willing it to stay still.

It was Layla. She had gotten to Ananth, too. Lord knew what poison she was filling his head with. Tara tried to soften her laboured breathing and strained to hear Ananth's reply. *Don't believe her, Ananth*, Tara prayed silently. *Don't you dare believe a word she says about me.*

"Now I know, so I'll be going," said Ananth. "Good night."

Tara heard footsteps. The back door closed softly and then there was silence. She continued sitting, paralyzed by what she had just seen and heard. What had Layla told Ananth about her?

Layla giggled. The giggle turned into soft laughter. Tara's insides burned as if she had swallowed a handful of fire. She got to her feet and crept closer. Layla was hurrying away, still chuckling to herself. A deep hatred flooded Tara, dousing the flames within.

"Stop right there!" said Tara.

Layla stopped and turned around slowly. Tara hurried up to her. In the moonlight, Layla's face looked like white marble except for eyes that were blacker than night and reminded Tara of deep, dark wells and endless tunnels.

"What're you doing here?" said Tara. Her voice was cold and stern — she hoped.

"What are *you* doing here?" said Layla.

"I heard you tell Ananth he should know something about me. What did you tell him?"

Layla stared at Tara, her face expressionless.

"Answer me, Layla, or I'll thrash you."

Layla smiled. Goosebumps rose on Tara's arms and she resisted the urge to back away.

"Just you try it, Tara. I'll cry so loudly and act so pitiful that the Panchayat will throw you out of Morni tonight. You're not very popular at the moment, so you better watch how you treat me."

Layla spoke quietly and with such confidence that Tara felt her own resolve shatter like a sheet of glass under a shower of hailstones. Tara stared at Layla, whom she had always despised and mostly ignored. But she couldn't ignore her now. She had to keep this snake close and observe her every move. Tara forced herself to look into her stepsister's eyes. Could Kali really be guiding her or was Layla's deep-rooted hatred showing itself now? Would a softer approach work with her?

"Layla, please!" said Tara. She took a step forward, though every muscle and every nerve recoiled at the thought. She cupped Layla's face with her hands. "Look, I didn't hurt your mother deliberately. She came after me. I had no choice. I was going to bring her back to Morni, *to you*. She didn't have a very easy time with Zarku. He was treating her very badly. In fact, she looked very relieved when it seemed that he was gone forever."

Layla stood listening intently, not moving away, but not saying a word, either. That was good; maybe this was the way to win her over: with kindness instead of threats.

"Tell me more," whispered Layla. "Tell me everything."

Tara forced herself to hold Layla's hand as they walked to the edge of the courtyard. They sat on the low mud wall and Tara continued with the story, skillfully weaving together facts and embellishments.

"We were all recovering from the tornado that had whipped through the cave after Zarku collapsed. Kali was trying to help me, but then ... then we both realized that Zarku had not really died. He had possessed her instead. You know what that means, don't you Layla?"

"Tell me," said Layla, calmly. Helplessness swept through Tara. How could this child be so emotionless hearing about her mother's last few minutes on earth? The moonlight shining on her cold eyes revealed no sadness, no regret, nothing.

"That means Zarku was controlling your mother, the same way he did with Suraj. And the first thing he made her do was to rush right at me. To kill me."

Tara took a deep shuddering breath as she recalled those moments. The crushing weight of darkness, the deep chasm belching hot fumes, Kali running at her, the hyena snapping at her ankles, and the unshakable fear that it was the end.

"I had no choice," said Tara. "No choice at all."

"There is always a choice, Tara. You could have let my mother live. I didn't like your *story* one little bit. I'm going home." Layla stood up and brushed mud off her large backside.

"Is there nothing I can do to make up for it?" said Tara with great effort.

Layla was silent for a moment. The chirrup of lizards and the mournful howl of a stray dog were the only sounds that broke the silence of the night. "There is one thing you can do."

"What?" asked Tara, her heart thumping. Maybe Layla's animosity would stop if she co-operated a bit.

And life would return to normal, for her and all of Morni.

"I'll ask Rakaji to call a meeting tomorrow," said Layla. "If you can say you're sorry for having killed my mother in front of the entire village and leave Morni forever, I'll stop. My mother had to go through this humiliation and so must you."

Tara jumped to her feet. Layla was playing with her. The same sort of game Zarku had played. It was now clear that she had no intention of stopping. Not until she had driven Tara out of her own home and destroyed her family.

"Is this *your* idea or your mother's?" Tara said. She wanted to grab Layla's neck and shake her hard.

"What does it matter? We both want the same thing — to see you suffer. So will you leave Morni or not?

"Never," snapped Tara. "And I don't regret killing Kali at all. *Not one bit.*"

"In that case things are going to get a lot worse for you," said Layla. She waddled away as fast as she could. Tara raced after her and spun her around, her chest heaving.

"I'll find a way to stop you, Layla. Don't think for one minute I'll let you get away with this just because you're a child. I'll make sure the villagers see you for the snake you really are!"

"You?" said Layla and laughed. "There is only one person who can stop me now, Tara. The god of death."

seven

Secrets

Lord Yama! Why hadn't she thought of him before now? Impressed by her bravery, he had helped once. Maybe he would help again, especially when she explained to him what a menace Layla was. He would be doing them a huge favour ridding Morni— no, the *world* — of Layla.

Tara had kept the pearly, white conch she had used to summon him the last time. She had tucked it safely inside her cupboard a while ago. But was it still there and would it work?

Tara raced home, flitting through the shadows like a bat. A stray dog chased her for a short distance, snapping at her heels.

"Go away!" she growled suddenly.

The dog stood still his ears and tail drooping. Tara remembered the other stray; his huge eyes that had lit up at the sight of food and who had been killed shortly after. She felt sorry for being so mean. "I'll bring food another time," she whispered and flew on.

Tara reached the back door of her hut, chanting silently ... *let it be there ... please let it be there*. She tiptoed into the kitchen and straight through to the front room. The sound of deep, steady breathing filled the room, punctuated by an occasional snore from her father.

Tara went straight to the cupboard and opened it an inch at a time. The right door squeaked. Tara held her breath and looked from her father to her mother to Suraj. No one stirred.

If she could find the conch tonight, she could summon Lord Yama right away. They would be rid of Layla forever and she would be safe and so would Morni. She was sure that with Layla gone, their troubles would be over. Her plan had to work!

Finally, Tara got the cupboard door open without waking anyone. She rummaged through her clothes in darkness. Deeper and deeper, she reached until her fingertips brushed the back. She realized with a jolt that there was no conch. She examined each and every item of her clothing, feeling their pockets and folds. Nothing. Had she lost it? How could she have been so careless?

She wanted to wake up her mother and ask her if she had seen it. But how was she going to explain why she was looking for a shell in the middle of the night? She didn't dare tell her what she was going to use it for; Lord Yama had forbidden it.

Tara knelt and fingered Suraj's clothes next. The moonlight barely reached the interior of the cupboard even though she had opened the doors as wide as they would go. It was not in her brother's clothes, either. Panic seeped through her, making her arms and legs feel leaden. How could she have lost such a precious thing?

Then she remembered: any kind of shell was considered bad luck, and most people did not keep one in the house. What if her mother had thrown it out? Tara sat back on her haunches trying to sniff back tears of frustration. She needed that conch. Now!

I'll make you suffer. Layla's menacing whisper echoed in Tara's head. She shuddered and started rummaging through the clothes again. It had to be here. Maybe she hadn't looked carefully enough.

"Didi?" said a soft voice. Tara jumped. Suraj stood behind her, rubbing his eyes. "What are you doing?"

"Shhhh! Nothing. Go to sleep."

"But Didi, I want to help," he whispered. "What are you looking for?"

"Something I lost. Now go to sleep or you'll wake Mother and Father."

"I'll find it for you," he said, leaning closer to whisper in her ear. "What did you lose?"

Tara sighed. Could she trust him enough to tell him what it was? And how many more questions would that lead to? She stared into his eyes and made up her mind.

"I'm looking for a shell, a pearly, white conch shell that was given to me by a … ummm … a friend. Do you know where it is?"

"Yes."

Tara's stomach churned. Was he serious? Just then a thought occurred to her and she frowned. "I kept it in the cupboard behind my clothes. Did you touch it without my permission?"

Suraj shook his head.

"You better be telling the truth!" whispered Tara. "Or I'll be very, very angry with you."

Suraj slid his hand into hers, glancing at their parents. Surprisingly they were still asleep. He tiptoed to the kitchen, pulling Tara behind him, and shut the door. She stared at Suraj in the dim moonlit room. Already, the baby features she loved so much were melting away, but his eyes held the same warmth and mischief. He and Layla were the same age, but like earth and sky when it came to personalities.

"You remember how we used to wake up early like this when Kali was around?" said Suraj. "You'd make us some tea and we'd talk before starting the day's work."

"Yes and don't remind me," said Tara. "It wasn't a good time."

"No, it wasn't," he said, as he helped himself to water from the earthen pot. The cup scraped the bottom and she remembered that they would soon have a long trek ahead of them to get water. Just the thought of it made her tired.

"So where is the conch and how do *you* know where it is?" demanded Tara. She spoke a little more loudly, now that they were out of earshot of their parents.

Suraj opened the back door and for the second time that night, Tara stepped out. Pale pink cracks had appeared in the blue-black slab of sky. Suraj went straight to a corner of the courtyard. He pointed to a sapling with broad, oval-shaped leaves and rounded tips that stood straight and tall, a peepul tree. At its base was her shell, splattered with mud. No wonder Tara hadn't noticed or recognized it!

She snatched it up and shook off the dew and mud that clung to it. Would it still work? Did the power go away if it became muddy?

"How did it get here?" Tara almost snapped at Suraj.

"Mother found it when she was clearing out the cupboard a few days ago. She asked me if it was mine and I said no. Then she said that *you* should have more sense than to bring a shell indoors — it's bad luck. Mother told me to throw it out immediately, but it was so beautiful that I decided to put it next to my peepul tree. Good idea, no?"

Tara smiled. "*Very* good idea, Suraj. A friend gave me this special shell. I'm so happy we found it."

"Which friend?"

"You wouldn't know him."

"What's his name?"

"I told you, Suraj, you don't know him. I — er — I met him when I wandering around in the forest the time I thought you were … gone."

"At least tell me his name."

"Um ... Amay," she said, watching him closely to see if he would figure it out.

Suraj scrunched up his face, then shook his head. "No, don't know him."

"Told you," said Tara. "Thanks for helping me find this. Now you better go back inside. It's almost morning. I'll give Mother a surprise and clean up the courtyard." What she really wanted to do was to clean up the shell and try it out. It was the one thought that burned inside her, but she dared not do it in front of Suraj or anyone else.

"I'll help, too," said Suraj. "I'm not sleepy. Should I get water from the well?"

Tara shook her head. "Can't go there, remember? Today we'll have to walk all the way to Pinjaur for water."

Suraj's face became serious. "Everyone will hate walking so far. And it's so hot."

Tara nodded. As of this morning when people replenished their stock of drinking water, the hardship would start and they would all be blaming her, hating her. It was more important than ever that she get rid of Layla fast, before she spread any more lies or did any more damage.

Their neighbour stepped out into her courtyard, balancing a pot on her head. Another rested against her hip.

"Good morning, Poonamji," Tara called out. "You're up very early."

The only answer they got was the tinkling of Poonam's anklets as she walked away. She did not even look in their direction when just a couple of days ago she had leaned over the low mud wall that separated their houses and passed over a steaming aloo-paratha for them to sample. She had even supported Tara when Raka had read out her punishment for desecrating the temple.

"Arre, Poonamji," said Suraj running up to the wall. "Did we do something to make you mad?"

Poonam had reached the edge of the courtyard. She looked back, glared at both of them, and walked away.

Tara sighed as Suraj returned, his shoulders slumped. "Why won't she talk to me? What have *I* done?"

Tara looked at Suraj's white expression and her heart ached for him. He was suffering because of her. Soon it would be the entire family.

"Layla started all this," said Suraj. "I hate her. I want her to go away and never come back."

For once Tara did not correct or chide him. Instead, she hugged him. "I know, Suraj. And I'm going to do something about her. Don't you worry."

"What are the two of you up to?" said Parvati. She stood by the back door, stifling a yawn.

"We were looking …" Suraj started to say and Tara nudged him.

"At the sunrise," she completed.

Parvati looked shrewdly from one to the other. "*Sunrise?*"

86

Tara casually slipped the conch into her pocket and nodded.

"And you, too?" she asked, her eyes shifting to Suraj.

Suraj nodded vigorously.

Parvati raised an eyebrow. "Well if you both have finished admiring the sunrise, I suggest you come in and have breakfast. Then you'll both have to get water from the next village. I'll go with your father to see how best we can clean up our own well."

As soon as she was gone, Tara knelt in front of Suraj. "Tell no one about this conch. It's our secret. All right? Promise me?" She stuck her palm out and Suraj laid his hand on it.

"Didi, I have a secret to share, too."

Tara stared into his face, trying to hide her dismay. When did her baby brother become old enough for secrets? "What is it?" she said.

"Promise you won't tell anyone?" He stuck his little palm out and Tara covered it with hers.

She then followed as Suraj raced to a corner of their courtyard where bits of stone, shattered clay pots, and other odds and ends were lying in a heap. Their mother had always meant to clear it away, but there was never enough time. Suraj reached into the middle of the pile of debris and pulled something out. He handed it to Tara..

The package was carelessly wrapped in oilskin and surprisingly heavy. "What is it, Suraj?"

"Open it and see," said Suraj. "But you can tell no one about it. Okay, Didi?"

Tara glanced behind her. Their mother was nowhere in sight. She unwrapped the parcel, and almost dropped it. In her hand lay Zarku's dagger. The one he was going to use to cut her heart out. The stones on its handle gleamed like red eyes in the early morning sunlight. The silver blade ended in a cruel, sharp tip. Tara re-wrapped the parcel with shaking hands and thrust it back into the middle of the pile.

"Where did you get this?" she asked, trying to steady her voice.

"In the cave," said Suraj. "While Sadia and I were waiting for you I saw this lying on the ground. I decided to take it."

"Why?" asked Tara. "Why did you take it?" She almost screamed at him, fighting the urge to shake him hard. What was he thinking?

Suraj shrugged. "I don't know. I just cannot remember. All I know is that I had to take it and keep it hidden. A voice inside my head told me to do it."

Tara lunged forward and clasped Suraj's face. She turned it up to the sun and ran her fingertips over his forehead. It was smooth, with not the tiniest little bump. She hugged him tight, relief flooding her, turning instantly to panic.

Why had he taken the dagger? But more important, *who* had told him to take it?

— eight —

The Untouchables

Tara and Suraj trudged the long and dusty road to Pinjaur. Along the way, they ran into a couple of villagers from Morni who ignored them. It was happening sooner than she had expected; they were all being treated like untouchables. For the first time, Tara realized how Gayatri-ma must feel — shunned through no fault of hers, treated as if she did not exist. And she did not like it one little bit.

The earth baked in the late morning sun. Large cracks had opened up on its surface like cuts on a wound that were crying out for salve. Tara looked up at the sky. There wasn't a ghost of a cloud in sight. Rain was the only thing that would heal the earth and cool the raging tempers of the villagers. But it would not happen today. Her throat was parched and she tried very hard not to think of a large glass of cool well water.

"How are we going to stop Layla?" said Suraj suddenly.

Tara shot a glance at him. It was the one thought that had nagged her constantly since last night.

"I'll think of something," said Tara. "Don't you worry about it."

"It has something to do with the shell, right?"

Tara met his eyes, trying to keep her face blank. How perceptive he'd become! But Lord Yama had warned her against telling anyone and that included Suraj. Before she could reply, someone called out.

"Tara, Suraj, wait up."

Tara whirled around. Ananth! He was still speaking to her. Whatever Layla had told him, it hadn't worked. She was so relieved that she almost dropped the earthen pot as she murmured a prayer. Ananth's support meant so much to her.

They waited while he caught up to them. He, too, was carrying an earthen pot. Tara gazed at her older brother, taller than her now, with deep, black eyes and dark hair cropped so close to his scalp that he almost looked bald. He'd even pierced his ear recently and a flash of silver caught her eye. Tara realized that she hadn't even noticed when he'd done it.

"I didn't want Mother to walk all the way to Pinjaur," said Ananth, holding up the pot he was carrying. "So I offered to get the water."

Tara smiled. "We could use some company."

They walked in silence on the dirt path that ran

between the paddy fields linking the village of Morni with Pinjaur. Sickly yellow crops raised their parched heads to the sky. Tara could not bear to look at them. Even if the rains came now, she knew in her heart that it was too late. The crop was lost and they would have to go hungry this year. If they were lucky, next year they would have a bountiful crop and eat well. She turned her eyes away from the swathe of yellow on either side and instead watched Suraj as he ran ahead, whipping the weeds lining the path with a supple branch.

"Are you all right?" said Ananth. "You don't seem yourself."

"Do you care?" Tara couldn't resist saying. "You haven't been around too often. Hope you're not starting to believe Layla's lies."

Ananth stopped immediately. "Why would you say that?"

Tara stared at him. His surprise seemed genuine. Should she tell him that she'd seen Layla talking to him last night? The words were crowding the tip of her tongue, dying to leap out. Finally Tara decided to stay silent. If he wanted to, he would tell her about it. In fact, she was curious to see if he would confide in her as he used to.

"Just wondering," said Tara. She shrugged, but her heart thudded. They had been through so much together. The first time was when they had set off to seek her mother and grandfather. Then again when they'd slipped away to rescue Suraj, Rohan, and Sadia.

Ananth, whom she had declared her brother by tying a rakhi to his wrist, had always been the voice of calm and reason. A voice she sorely missed these days.

"Well, stop wondering," said Ananth. "If I haven't been around lately, it's because I'm worried about Mother. The villagers have started acting weird suddenly. I just cannot understand it. I'm so afraid they'll change their minds and decide that she should carry out … the Sati ceremony after all and then throw us out of the village."

His speech and his stride faltered. Tara knew why. Sati was when a widow was forced to burn on her husband's funeral pyre. Prabala had saved Gayatri-ma from this horrible fate a year ago. But with the villagers so superstitious these days, and Prabala gone, Ananth probably had cause to worry. Who knew what the angry, frightened villagers might do?

"The villagers are mad," said Tara, voicing her thoughts. "I wish the monsoons would come soon. Then all my problems would be solved, except the one called Layla."

"Speaking of Layla, you should know that your dear stepsister stopped by last night."

Tara exhaled slowly, trying not to let the relief show. He was confiding in her once again! Nothing had changed between them.

"Why?" said Tara trying to keep her voice light, unconcerned. "What did she want?"

"She wanted me to stay away from you," said Ananth. "She said that great harm would befall me and my mother, if we continued to associate with you. You and your family were like the plague, and were to be avoided. I think she was struggling to find a name for it."

Tara glanced at him as they continued to walk. His eyes were smiling and his lips twitched. It seemed like old times when he used to tease her. Was it her overactive imagination that made her think he'd been mad at her the evening of the feast?

"*I* would have called it Tara-itis!" said Ananth in a serious voice. "The deadly plague."

Tara stared at him for a moment and then burst into giggles. "Taritis."

Ananth laughed so loud and hard that Suraj ran back toward them. "What's so funny?" he asked. "Tell me, *tell me*!"

"There's a new plague in town, did you know?" said Ananth amid hoots of laughter.

Tara held a stitch in her side. "It's called Taritis and it's contagious," she said, still giggling.

"Once you get it, there's no cure," said Ananth, barely able to speak, he was laughing so hard. "Taritis stays with you until you *die*!"

"No cure at all," echoed Tara.

Suraj looked from one to the other, completely confused. Both she and Ananth were now completely immobilized with laughter.

"You're both mad," he said and walked away in a huff.

• • •

"Couldn't you have managed to get two pots of water?" said Parvati. "I've used up most of the water for cooking. And we'll need some to last us until tomorrow morning."

"Only one pot per family was allowed," said Tara.

Suraj nodded. "Someone tried to take two pots and he was almost beaten up."

Tara folded a piece of chappati and scooped up some brinjal and potato. Her eyes watered as the spices hit her tongue and she took a large gulp of cool well water.

"Why are they rationing water in Pinjaur?" said Shiv. He stopped chewing his food and looked from Suraj to Tara.

"They said their water was also running low and though they were glad to help, they had to ration it until the monsoon arrived," said Tara. "So they posted a villager there to make sure no one took more than one pot."

Parvati sighed deeply as she dipped a steel tumbler into the pot. It scraped the bottom sounding like nails scratching a wall. "One glass of water left and it has to last us until tomorrow morning."

Tara was immediately thirsty again. She wanted to drink water till she was ready to burst, but knew she'd have to be content with a sip at most. The hot kitchen and spicy food made her sweat profusely. She pushed away her plate which still had some remaining food.

"Don't you even think of wasting food, Tara. Things are going to get even tougher once the crops fail. You will eat properly while we can still afford a decent meal."

Her mother's words made her cringe; there was so much truth in them. Shiv and Suraj had finished every morsel of food and even wiped their thalis clean with a last bit of chappati. Tara pulled the thali back toward her and gulped down the food, tasting only hopelessness and fear.

That night Tara could not sleep, she lay awake trying to count sheep. It didn't work. She closed her eyes and breathed deeply, thinking of blue skies, lush, green paddy fields, and a shimmering lake of water, trying to calm a mind that had been scurrying all day like a trapped rat.

"It's a good thing you stayed at home today," said Shiv softly. "It got pretty ugly, but I didn't want to mention it in front of the children."

Tara held her breath. They thought she was asleep. Suraj was breathing evenly and she tried to imitate him.

"What happened?" said Parvati, a catch in her voice.

"The cleaning up of the well started, but when I tried to help, Raka sent me away.

"Why? What does he think you'll do?"

"I don't know," said Shiv. The mournful tone of his voice made Tara sick. "He told me to go home. Most of our friends barely talked to me. Drona told me to leave the village along with my family. He said that *we* were the cause of all this misfortune and the sooner we left, the better for us all."

Tara gasped and remembered too late; she was supposed to be fast asleep.

The cot creaked and she heard Parvati get out of bed. Tara tried to breathe deeply when her mother's warm breath fanned her face. A moment ticked by, then another. Tara opened an eye and saw her parents staring at her. Shiv had his arms folded across his chest.

"You might as well open the other eye, too," said Parvati. She tried to sound angry, but looked too tired to make a real effort.

"How much did you hear?" said Shiv.

Tara sat up. "All of it."

"Come on, let's talk in the kitchen over a cup of tea —" Parvati said and stopped.

"There's no water for tea," said Tara. "I know."

They all trooped into the kitchen and sat down. "Things are really bad for us, right, Father?" said Tara.

"Yes, my child. In hard times, the villagers need an excuse; anything or anyone they can blame for their calamities. It wouldn't be so bad for us if it hadn't been for Layla. She's taking advantage of this situation and fanning the fires of discontent."

"I wish *my* father were here," said Parvati. "He would have put an end to this madness once and for all. The villagers respect him and would have listened to him no matter what the circumstances."

"Then I'll get Prabala back," said Shiv. "I'll leave at dawn."

"Where will you go?" asked Tara. "He could be anywhere."

"To the Himalayas," said Shiv. "I'm sure people will have heard of him. I'll ask around and follow his trail."

"If only I could tell you exactly where he was," said Parvati, "but I can't. I just don't know."

"Mother, you were able to predict the future at one time," said Tara. "Can you not try to see where Grandfather is? It would make it so much easier for Father to find him."

"It's no use, Tara. I've lost my gift. Often the villagers would curse me for seeing into the future. When I told Kali about her husband's death, she disowned me as a friend. I wished then, with all my heart, that I did not have such a terrible gift. I did not realize it, but already the gift was getting weaker." She was silent for a moment, staring into space. "The gods were taking away my *sight* because I could not appreciate it."

Outside a dog howled and Tara remembered the mutilated stray. It made her queasy.

"Remember when we were going back to Morni to face Zarku, I couldn't see anything then, either?" said Parvati. "I thought it was because of Zarku's evil that had cloaked the village, but now I know it was also because I was not meant to see. That I had finally lost the power. And I regret it immensely now. The one time I need this sight the most, I don't have it."

Parvati buried her face in her hands and sobbed. Tara felt a pang of fear. Her mother was normally the rock of the family. If she floundered what would become of them?

"Mother, don't," said Tara. She crawled over and hugged her tight.

Shiv moved closer and put his arms around them both. "I wouldn't give up hope just yet, Parvati. I'll find Prabala and return as soon as I can. All you have to do is lay low and stay safe. I'll be back before you know it."

Parvati wiped her eyes with the edge of her saree and sniffed. She attempted to smile. "You're right, both of you. I'm lucky to have such a brave family. All right, Shiv. You go find Prabala and we'll keep Morni at bay until you return." Her lips trembled and she clamped them together; a sure sign that she was very upset.

Tara knew the villagers could be merciless. She still remembered how angry they were with Kali during her trial. If the Panchayat had not decided to banish her they probably would have stoned her to death as they did in the olden times. She'd also heard snatches of whispered conversations about other terrible punishments for those found guilty of crimes against the village; tongues being cut off, people being burned alive, and another rumour where an entire family had been thrown alive into a pit of venomous snakes. Yes, the villagers could be ruthless if they decided that Tara and her family were a threat to Morni!

Back in bed, Tara still could not sleep. What if her father could not find Prabala and wandered for an eternity. What if things went badly wrong while he was away? Where would they go looking for *him*?

There was only one option. Tara slipped her hand into her pocket, her fingers closing over the conch shell.

Lord Yama. She had to summon him. Tonight.

nine

The God of Death

Tara slipped out the back door. A faint breeze caressed her cheek as it wafted past. It was a little cooler outside and she missed sleeping under a canopy of stars.

If only she could get Lord Yama to agree to help her tonight, her father would not have to leave. This would also mean that she would have to tell her father *everything*, but she'd worry about it later. First she had to see if the conch still worked!

Tara slipped out of the courtyard. It was long past midnight and all of Morni slumbered. Not even a stray dog wandered the dusty lanes between the huts. A pale moon lit the way as she ran straight through the village, toward the forest, alive with hoots, grunts, and growls. She stopped at the edge for a moment, took a deep breath, and plunged in.

After a few moments, Tara halted near a clump of trees, huddled together as if sharing a secret. She could still see the shadows of the huts behind her. It gave her a bit of relief; she wasn't too far from safety.

She took the conch out of her pocket and stared at it. The faint light filtering in through the thick canopy of leaves lit up the creamy edges of the shell. *Let it work, please let it work*, she prayed. With trembling hands she raised it to her lips and blew hard.

The forest became silent. Wind sighed through the trees. An owl answered. There was no other sound except the beating of her heart.

Tara blew on the conch once more and strained her ears for the sounds that had streamed out of it the first time she'd called Lord Yama; the crashing of waves, the silvery tinkling, the thundering of horse's hooves.

Nothing.

Tara stared at the conch, fighting the panic bubbling up from a deep reservoir within her. Had the conch lost its powers? Had she made Lord Yama angry by mistreating his precious gift? *Forgive me, Lord*, Tara prayed. *I didn't even know when Mother threw it out!*

Tara shook the conch. There was a faint rattling from inside. She moved out of the tree cover so that the sickly moon afforded some light and shook the conch again. Bits of gravel poured out onto her palm. She rattled it until the sound stopped, and blew hard one last time, her lungs burning for air.

Tara peered through the trees, trying to penetrate the deep gloom of the forest. Something slithered past her foot, rustling the carpet of dead leaves. She froze, watching a shiny black cobra glide through the undergrowth and stop a short distance away. Was this a sign? She stared at it to see if it would act strangely, or try and communicate with her in some way.

The cobra raised its hood. Its forked tongue flickered in and out. It swayed gently, turning its hood this way and that, tasting the air.

"Mother," said Tara. "Is that you?"

The cobra whipped round and looked straight at her. It hissed.

A cold chill trickled down Tara's spine; if this was a real cobra, she should be running in the opposite direction, not trying to talk to it.

Leaves rustled behind her and Tara's pulse raced. She had to use every ounce of discipline to avoid any sudden moves. She turned her head slowly to see if it was just another animal searching for dinner, or the cobra's mate.

The cobra tasted the air again and then dived at Tara's feet, a blur of silvery-black. She screamed and jumped aside, her heart thundering in her chest. But the cobra had no interest in her. It was after the animal she had heard rooting in the undergrowth; a large mongoose.

The mongoose grunted at the cobra as they circled one another. In spite of her fear, Tara watched, fascinated, as age-old enemies thrust and parried skillfully, each with their own particular strengths. The mongoose was larger and heavier of the two, but the cobra was smart and supple.

On and on the fight went as they grappled with each other. At times it seemed the cobra didn't have a chance. But then the tables would turn and the snake would have the upper hand. And suddenly, before Tara even realized what was happening, the cobra sank its fangs into the mongoose's neck. It gave a high-pitched shriek, twitched, and lay still. The fight was over. The cobra, in spite of being smaller, had won.

Tara realized she had stuffed her knuckles into her mouth and had been gnawing on them. She wiped her hands on her kurta and looked around. Too much time had passed. Lord Yama was not coming. Whatever plan she came up with, she would have to do it on her own.

The cobra uncoiled itself from around the mongoose and slipped away. Somehow, watching it gave her hope. Layla may be formidable, but she, *Tara,* had the brains. She would figure out a way and win.

Tara looked at the conch. It was useless now and yet she couldn't bear to throw it away. She turned to go when she heard muffled steps. Something heavy was approaching. She pressed her back against the trunk of a sal tree as the sound changed direction; first from the left, then the right, then from behind her. It seemed as if a drunken elephant were making its way toward her.

The thuds grew louder. Tara couldn't stand it a moment longer. She sprinted toward the treeline and to the safety of Morni.

"You call me and then run away, Tara?" said a deep voice. "I didn't expect that from you."

Tara stopped, turned around. There was Lord Yama, astride his bull, his black mace slung over his shoulder. A faint glow emanated from his massive green frame so that, in spite of the darkness, she saw him clearly.

"You came," said Tara. She rushed back and stood close, not daring to touch him or the bull. "You heard my call and came. Oh, thank you, Lord!"

"I knew that you wouldn't call me unless you were in dire need," said Lord Yama. "What is it, child?"

Now that he was here, Tara didn't know where to start. "I … we … need your help, Lord Yama. We need you to take Layla away from the village."

"*Take?*" said Lord Yama. His voice was like a whiplash. "What do you mean by *take?* There is only one way I can take anyone from earth and that is if they die. Surely you know that, Tara."

Tara shivered, wondering if she had made the wrong decision by calling him. Once she spoke her mind, there was no going back. Would the god of death take kindly to being ordered around by a mere mortal, a child? Already it seemed as if he was mad at her.

"I know that, Lord," said Tara. She knelt and pressed her palms together, hoping there were no more snakes lurking close by. "And that is why, I humbly request for you to ... to kill Layla and take her away from here."

The silence was so loud, it was deafening. Even the forest seemed to be holding its breath. Lord Yama glared at Tara and she gazed back at him, trying her hardest not to look away.

"Are you suggesting that I kill someone just to suit your convenience, Tara? Could you really be that naive?" he said in a terribly calm voice. "Or that selfish?"

"Lord Yama, please forgive me. If there were any other choice, I would not have called you. But Layla has become a terrible menace. She has been creating nothing but havoc and trouble for me —"

"Ahhh, I see," he said. "Layla is being mean to poor Tara. She is unhappy and so she calls on the god of death to take away the problem. Is that it? I am very disappointed in you! Return my conch immediately. You will never summon me again."

"No!" said Tara. "No, it's not like that at all. It's just that ... please let me explain, Lord. You're scaring me and I'm not able to think straight. It might also help if you stopped glaring at me."

Tara wrung her hands, looking up at Lord Yama, wondering if she had gone too far. Suddenly, he threw his head back and laughed. "Tara, you haven't lost your spirit, I can see that. It's what makes you so endearing and allows you to get away with admonishing the Lord of Death, whom most mortals fear to set eyes upon." He slid off the bull, rested his mace against a tree and sat on a rock. "Does this meet with your approval?" He said it very seriously but his eyes were smiling.

Tara sat at his feet and poured out the whole story, starting with Kali and Zarku and working her way up to Layla's antics. When she fell silent, Lord Yama got to his feet and paced. The bull stood patiently to one side, flicking its tail now and then to drive away the incessant flies.

"Hmmmm," said Lord Yama. He stopped, looked at Tara, and resumed pacing again. Under her, the forest floor trembled.

Tara followed him with her eyes, a million questions fighting to burst out of her mouth. But she held them in. First, Lord Yama had to decide whether he was going to help her or not. *But he had to*, she prayed silently. *He must!*

Finally Lord Yama sat on the stone once again. "Tara, I have given this a lot of thought. I understand your pain. There are people in this world who, like Layla, bring misery to all who know them. But Lord Brahma, the Creator, had a reason for putting them there and I cannot go against him, against nature, and take away their life without just cause. Do you understand what I'm saying?"

"But, Lord, what if the person is really evil, and, through her actions, more lives are lost? Is it not right then to take one life and save countless others?"

"A very good argument, Tara, but I still cannot do what you ask of me. As I said, I can only take away the soul of a dead person. I *cannot* and *will not* kill them. I'm sorry but I cannot help you."

Tara gazed at him, angry and disappointed. How could he talk of rules when this one *child* could destroy Morni? He had to help her and she knew what she had to do next. She had hoped she wouldn't have to use that argument, but she had no choice.

"You promised to dispose of Zarku's ashes, which my grandfather, Prabala, sealed in an urn," said Tara. "How did it fall into Kali's hands? Because of it, Zarku was able to come back. He almost killed my brother and we lost Rohan. You're responsible for his death, Lord Yama."

Deafening silence returned. Lord Yama sprang to his feet and towered over Tara, glaring at her. She met his gaze, trying not to flinch or look away. Whether he liked it or not, it was the truth!

"How dare you blame me!" said Lord Yama. The air around them crackled with anger. "Yes, I said I'd dispose of Zarku's ashes, but one of my helpers slipped up. By the time he came to collect the urn, it was gone."

"I'm not *blaming* you, Lord," said Tara. "Merely pointing out the truth of the matter. If you cannot help me, then tell me who can. I have to stop Layla somehow, even if I have to kill her myself!"

"Be careful of what you say, Tara. Taking someone's life is a serious matter, especially if that someone is a child! You will end up in the Underworld from where there is no escape. For eternity."

"Then what am I supposed to do?" shrieked Tara. "Watch this *child* destroy my family? Morni? Everyone I love? There has to be something you can do to help me."

Lord Yama's expression softened. "There is one other way," he said and gazed at her for a long moment. "But it's very ... no, forget it." He shook his massive head. "I should never have mentioned it. I must go. There are many matters that await my attention. Good luck, Tara. These things have a way of sorting themselves out. Trust in the pattern that our Creator has laid out for each of us. All you need is patience."

Tara jumped to her feet. "Please, Lord Yama. That's what Mother says, but I just can't sit around and do nothing. You have to tell me. Whatever it is, I can do it."

Yama looked deep into her eyes; it seemed he was looking into her very soul. "I believe you, Tara, Your bravery is unsurpassed. I have yet to see a child as courageous as you. But ... are you brave enough to face your own death?"

It felt as if someone had emptied a bucket of ice-cold water over her. "What-what did you say?" Tara was sure she had misheard him.

"Can you face your own death to save your family and your village?" said Yama watching her shrewdly.

"I don't understand?"

"Well, like I said, there is a way," said Yama. "I can take you to the one person who can tell you how to stop Layla; her mother Kali. But to do that I must take you to her — in the Underworld."

"I'm not afraid of that. I'll do it!" said Tara, though the thought of seeing Kali again made her break out in a cold sweat.

"I've no doubt you can do it," said Yama. He sat down again and beckoned to Tara. She sat at his feet. "It's what happens after."

"What … happens after?" asked Tara, searching his face. She knew in her heart she would not like his answer.

"The rule is that once you go to the Underworld, you cannot come back to the world of the living. I will make an exception in your case and give you twenty-four hours on earth to take care of Layla. But then you must return with me. You will be dead to your family, but you will live the rest of your life in the Underworld, neither dead, nor alive."

Tara sat very still as Lord Yama's words went around and around in her head like a dog chasing its tail; *you will live the rest of your life in the Underworld; neither dead, nor alive.*

Neither dead, nor alive.

She stared at the ground for a long time, not really seeing it. All of the choices that faced her were incredibly hard. She didn't want Layla's death on her hands. The price of talking to Kali to stop her daughter was too heavy. And the last option was patience, which could prove fatal for her and her family. A heavy hand rested on her shoulder and she started.

"It's a huge shock," said Lord Yama. "I know. No one wants to die and especially not someone as young as you! I have taken many children kicking and screaming to the Underworld. Children who died unnatural deaths or those who were killed. They did not want to leave their parents. They wanted to remain in the same house forever. It's one of the hardest parts of my job and a sad one."

"Children who were killed?" said Tara. "Why do they need to be in the Underworld? It's not their fault that they died young."

"For a short time only," said Lord Yama. "Until we determine the cause of death. Sometimes they die young because of the terrible sins they committed in their previous lives. Once it is determined that they are innocent, they are sent to a better, kinder place."

Tara nodded, not really understanding. Her own death loomed large in her mind. "But why can't I meet Kali in the Underworld and come back," she said. "After all, I'm going there by choice, for the good of the people of Morni and —"

"Stop right there," said Lord Yama in a firm voice. "I've told you the rules and you'll just have to abide by them. There is no bargaining here."

Around them, darkness was melting away and dawn was approaching. If she went with the Lord to talk to

Kali, she would die. But life was already quite unbearable for her. She dreaded each new day, wondering what unpleasant surprises would spring forth from Layla's sick, twisted mind.

"I have to go, Tara. Are you coming?"

"No." The word flew from her lips unbidden. "No," she repeated softly. "I have so much more I have to do here. How can I leave my family and just give up ... I'm sorry, but no." She stared up at Lord Yama, expecting to see anger or disapproval because of her weakness. Instead she saw sadness.

He patted her head. "Tara, I understand. It's tough to think of dying at thirteen. But I respect your decision and your honesty. Best of luck with your fight against Layla."

"You're leaving?"

"You can't have Death hanging around you all the time, Tara. You'll get a bad reputation," said Yama. He smiled, and, in spite of everything, Tara smiled, too.

"If I were to change my mind, can I call you?"

Yama looked stern again. "Tara, I have much work to do and many souls to take to the Underworld. I cannot be summoned on a whim. Do you understand?"

"Yes. I'm sorry."

"I know you called me out of concern for your family and the villagers so I will say no more. You are a brave, unselfish girl and I will always admire you, but there is a limit to what I will tolerate."

Tara took a deep breath and held out the conch to him. It was like giving up a part of her. What if she needed it again? Her hand shook and the conch, perched on her palm, jiggled. "Here, take it." She blinked back tears. This was so hard.

Yama closed her fingers over the conch. "I will leave this with you, Tara. But it will work only one more time, so use it wisely. Call only when you truly need me."

Tara clutched the shell to her breast. For now, the conch of death was with her and she felt an odd sense of relief.

"Good luck, Tara."

"Thank you, Lord Yama."

He patted her on the head, climbed onto his bull, and, before her eyes, faded into the morning mist shrouding the forest. She could hear the muffled clip-clopping of the bull's hooves, though she could not see him. The earth trembled under her feet and then was still. He was gone.

Tara ran back toward the village, and home. She stopped at the edge of the treeline. The horizon was outlined in gold. The sight brought tears to her eyes. How close she had come to never seeing another sunrise.

She remembered the fight between the mongoose and the cobra. In spite of being mismatched, the snake had won.

And so would she.

ten

Fire!

Wisps of smoke were curling out the back door of their hut when Tara returned. She walked into the kitchen where Parvati and Shiv sat sharing a cup of tea.

"Where did you go?" they asked in unison. Worry had etched deep lines onto their faces. Tara wished she had returned before they awoke and spared them the anxiety.

"I-er —"

"Did you go to the temple again?" asked Shiv.

"Yes!" said Tara, silently begging forgiveness of Lords Ganesh and Yama for the lie. "I couldn't sleep, so I decided to sit there for a while."

Parvati patted a spot next to her. Tara sank to the ground gratefully, her mind in turmoil. Had she made the right decision in refusing to go with Lord Yama? What if that had been her only chance to stop Layla, apart from killing the girl herself?

Parvati put her arm around her daughter's shoulders and Tara sagged against her, gazing at the familiar surroundings that always calmed her. Silver vessels and thalis gleamed on the shelves, the blackened clay stove they used every day was covered with bits of ash, the heavy mortar and pestle her mother used to pound spices stood in a corner next to the earthen pots of drinking water. The fragrance of milky tea, wood smoke, and dung cakes wrapped her in their warm embrace. She would have missed all of this if she had gone to the Underworld.

And if she had left without telling her parents, they would have gone out of their minds with worry. No, she had made the right decision. There had to be another way to stop Layla and she would find it.

"Your father is leaving shortly," said Parvati. "It's a good thing you're up early; at least you'll get to bid him farewell." She busied herself packing some chappatis and leftover vegetables along with a small bottle of precious water and a couple of guava fruits.

"When will you be back, Father?"

"When I have found Prabala," he replied. "And, God willing, I'll find him soon." He gulped the last of his tea, tied a long red cloth into a turban around his head, and stood up.

They walked out the back door and into the courtyard. The sky was a rosy pink and birds trilled cheerfully. Tara wished they would shut up.

Parvati handed the bundle of food to Shiv. "May God be with you. Be careful and come back soon."

Tara flung her arms around her father and hugged him tight. She wanted him to carry the memory of her smiling face on his journey. But it was hard; tears swarmed her eyes and bubbled up inside her throat.

For these last two years, their life as a family had been doomed. First her mother and grandfather had left Morni to avoid the taunts of the villagers. Her mother had barely returned when Zarku had kidnapped Suraj. A hard-won fight had brought them together only to have her father leave again. Was this ever going to end? Would they ever live as a family for longer than a few days?

Yes, said the voice within her that she had come to trust. *Have faith and you will all be together again.* As Tara waved goodbye, she couldn't help wonder if it was the voice of reason or merely her deepest hope.

• • •

"Why has Shiv gone looking for Prabala?" asked Ananth. He picked up a moss-covered stone and chucked it into the undergrowth. It landed far away with a thump and crackle of leaves.

Tara didn't answer. She threw her stone, which landed barely a few feet away.

"You throw like a girl," said Ananth. "Useless."

"I am a girl!" growled Tara. Then she looked into his eyes and saw the twinkle.

They were sitting at the edge of the forest. The fierce rays of the afternoon sun beat down upon them, and, in spite of the shade of a sal tree, Tara felt as if she were sitting in a tandoor. A dry and dusty wind gusted through the trees, reeking of smoke, overripe fruit, and manure. Most of Morni slumbered in their huts; it was too hot to work in the fields and risk sunstroke.

Not a cloud marred the blue expanse above them.

"So, answer me!" said Ananth.

"You know why," said Tara. "The villagers are behaving badly toward me, and now they're shunning my family, too. When mother was able to look into the future, they drove her away, but when she and Prabala returned to help them out, they were sorry. And they're doing it all over again."

"They're scared," said Ananth. "There's been no rain. We've just managed to clean up our well and now have to wait for it to fill up again. And even then it might be too late for the crops. Morni is facing a very bad year and they need someone to blame."

"What about you?" said Tara. "Do you believe I'm bringing bad luck to the village?" She picked up a handful of dirt and let it trickle through her hands. She did it again and yet again. Finally Ananth spoke.

"Tara, you know I don't believe in superstitions. It makes my blood boil when they shun my mother just because she's a widow. *She's* the one suffering. I wish I could do something, anything to lessen their anger toward her! But you have to admit that a lot of terrible things have happened in Morni all at once. It was bound to cause some fear."

"But everyone is in the same boat," said Tara. "No village for miles around us has had rain. Their crops are failing, too."

"Yes, but they still have water. And no dead animal was found in any of their temples."

"You forget one *special* thing we have which no other village has," said Tara. She yanked a handful of weeds and shredded them into tiny pieces. "Layla."

"Oh come on, Tara. What can a child do?" said Ananth. "You're giving her way too much credit."

Tara stared at him. "You don't know her like I do, Ananth. I've lived with her. I know what she is capable of. She's evil and more dangerous than Kali because no one will take a child seriously. That is why she gets away with it. There's more ill-luck coming, I just know it."

"The heat's fried your brains, Tara. You're getting paranoid."

Tara shot to her feet. Sweat popped out from every pore with the exertion. "In that case, I won't trouble you any more and take my paranoid thoughts home where at least Suraj and my mother will listen to me. You've changed so much, Ananth. There was a time when you believed in me."

"Tara, wait. I didn't mean that. Don't go ... please."

Tara ignored him and kept walking.

"You're just acting childish," Ananth called out after her. "Stop throwing tantrums and come back." His voice had a hard edge to it.

Tara wanted to march back and slap his head for even suggesting it. She hoped he'd come running after her but he didn't. So she kept walking.

"All right, go!" said Ananth. "Don't come back later when you need to talk. I'll be too busy throwing a tantrum of my own to listen to you."

I don't need anyone, thought Tara as she strode home without a backward glance. The baked earth scorched the soles of her feet through her mojris. Her scalp prickled with heat. She prayed for rain, but the sky remained cloudless.

"Is that you, Tara?" Parvati called out from the kitchen as soon as she stepped into the hut.

"Yes, Mother."

"I hate to ask this now, but can you fetch another pot of water? The tulsi needed watering and I still have to fill Bela's bucket."

Anger pulsed within Tara at the thought stepping out once again into the searing afternoon heat, and walking two kilometres for a pot of water. Even the walk to their well would have been torture. All she wanted to do was put a cool cloth over her head and lie down.

"Do I have to go now?" asked Tara, trying hard not to let the anger spill into her voice.

Parvati appeared at the kitchen door. She looked hot, tired, and dishevelled. So unlike her usual self. "Yes. It's a long walk and I want you home before dark. That's why you have to go now." Her eyes were puffy and red.

Tara rushed forward and hugged her. "Of course I'll go."

"Be careful, Tara. It's far away and in this heat …"

"Don't worry. I'll take Suraj with me. We'll be fine," said Tara. "It's only for a few days anyway. Father will be back with Grandfather soon and then everything's going to be all right."

• • •

"Everything's going to be all right … everything's going to be all right …" Tara chanted the mantra softly over and over again as she lay on her cot, staring out at the patch of cloudless night framed by the window.

The air was so hot and heavy that even the thinnest of sheets was unbearable. She threw it off and fanned her face with the edge of her dupatta.

Tara relived her walk to Pinjaur that afternoon. The villagers had taken to whispering when she passed. Once she had caught the words, "Shiv" and "Prabala." So they knew her father had gone looking for him.

Something else nagged her like a persistant toothache. She squirmed on the cot, fanning herself harder. What was it? Tara had learned to follow her instincts and went over the day, slowly, carefully, trying to figure out why she felt so uneasy.

She and Suraj had managed to bring two pots of water, each from a different well, and painstakingly carried them back home over kilometres of dusty road. Tara had been so tempted to sit by the wayside and gulp it all down, but somehow she had restrained herself and so had Suraj. They allowed themselves a cup of water each when they finally staggered home, sweaty and pungent. Parvati had given them both a laddoo as a reward; a sweet moment that was over too soon!

Their stores were sufficient for a few weeks, though their mother was being very careful with the food. The village grocer still sold vegetables to them and they had been able to supplement these with the harvest from their vegetable patch at the back of the house. But with the intense heat and lack of water, the brinjals, beans, and potatoes were shrivelling fast.

All they could do now was to wait for Shiv and Prabala to return. "Keep a low profile," her mother had instructed her at dinnertime. "And stay out of Layla's way!"

Layla! *That* was what was bothering her. Her skin prickled at the thought of her stepsister. Layla had not been near them since the last chat at the temple, preferring to stay with Rakaji and Sumathy, who had believed her lies and taken her in.

Tara knew that this was far from over, but try as she might, she could not figure out what Layla or Kali would dream up next. She dozed at long last, trying to ignore the oppressive heat, the terrible thirst clawing at her throat, the coir of the cot biting into her back, and her clothes stinking of acrid sweat.

She wandered through the barren land. There were no trees or huts. Huge boulders dotted the landscape. Cliffs stood like sentinels in the distance. A red sun lay dying on the horizon, its lifeblood staining sky, earth, and even her hands, a vivid crimson.

She was all alone.

"Over here, Tara," someone called out. She whirled around. The landscape was still deserted. Where was the caller hiding? The sun sank lower. Shadows slithered over the rocks. They came from every direction now, converging on Tara, lapping at her heels with black tongues.

"Here, Tara."

The voice seemed to be coming from a crevice between two large boulders, a fissure darker than night. And very narrow. She ran toward it.

"Anyone in there?" asked Tara. "Come out where I can see you."

"Come in, I'm waiting," someone said. She thought she recognized the voice, the name hovered at the edge of her memory, elusive as smoke.

Tara looked around her. The shadows had all but devoured the light. Sullen stars hung in the inky sky. They seemed to be glaring down at her, unrelenting in their gaze. A cold wind caressed her cheek.

Tara stepped into the crevice and started walking. The narrow walls grazed her arms, a dank smell filled her nose. Deeper and deeper she walked. "Are you still there?" she asked. "Show yourself."

"It's over, Tara," said the familiar voice. "For you and your family." Then there was silence.

A trap! She had to get out! Tara turned to leave. A wall of flames erupted in front of her, growing taller and fiercer, reaching for the sky. She screamed and turned around. Fire behind her, too. Fingers of flame reached out for her, scorching her skin. Smoke filled her nose and her lungs, choking her.

"*Help!*" Tara shrieked.

"*Help!*" a voice echoed hers. "*Fire!*"

Tara's eyes flew open. In front of her was a crackling wall of fire. Flames shot out, singing her skin. Had Lord Yama transported her to the Underworld already or was she in a very real dream? She stared at the flames, paralyzed by the orange and red swirling within its depths.

"TARA, MOVE!" Parvati shrieked.

And then it hit her; their hut was aflame. It wasn't a dream at all.

Tara jumped off the cot and ran to her mother, who stood in the centre of the room, hugging Suraj. The fire was all around them, greedily feeding on their home, growing taller and wider. Any moment it would devour them, too.

"What do we do?" said Suraj, gripping her hand. "We're all going to die."

Parvati stared at the fire, mesmerized. Black smoke billowed up and they coughed and choked, trying to draw breath. Tara snatched her dupatta off the cot. "Cover your mouth with this," she said throwing it at Suraj. Flames were licking at the walls, moving rapidly toward the back of the hut.

"Let's go through the kitchen," said Tara. "We can make it."

She willed her legs to move, but they refused. Another cloud of smoke filled the room as a corner of the hut gave way. Tara lost all sense of direction.

"This way," yelled Parvati. "Follow me, Tara. Don't dawdle."

Just then, the roof caught fire and burning straw rained down on them. Parvati ran toward the back of the hut, pulling Suraj along.

"Mother, wait!" yelled Tara. But Parvati didn't hear her. Tara watched in horror as a large piece of burning roof fell straight on to Suraj. A huge chunk of beam crashed down seconds later.

Both Suraj and Parvati screamed and then were silent. Her heart pounding, Tara ran around the burning beam, fanning the air. Suraj lay still on the floor, covered with embers. His clothes were starting to smoulder. Parvati was on her knees, coughing and retching. A large gash on her forehead oozed blood.

"Tara," she gasped. "Run. Save yourself and Suraj."

Tara felt her consciousness slipping away. Smoke filled her lungs with every breath, clouding all coherent thought. It would be easier just to give up and die. She coughed so hard, it seemed as if her heart would pop out of her mouth.

Yes, said a voice. *Give up. If you don't, I'll just keep at it*. It was the same voice she had heard in her dream. Layla's voice. Tara saw her face clearly now; smiling, nodding. *Give up*, said Layla. *Or I'll get you some other way*.

"No!" yelled Tara. "You won't win, Layla. I won't let you."

She dragged Suraj from the charred heap of wood and straw and beat the smouldering patches on his clothes with her bare hands. He was unconscious, which was good. He would be easier to handle. The flames had reached the door between the main room and the kitchen. A few seconds more and that escape route would be blocked, too.

Tara pulled Suraj to his feet and threw him over her shoulder. She staggered as his dead weight settled on her. *Give up*, Layla's voice taunted her.

Tara tottered over to Parvati, who was still on the floor, her face streaming with blood from the gash on her forehead.

"Mother, come on," said Tara. She tugged at her.

Parvati looked at her with a blank expression.

"Mother, I've got Suraj, let's go!" Tara screamed so loud this time that Parvati snapped out of her daze. She scrambled to her feet. They dodged more bits of fiery roof and ran the few steps towards the doorway. Golden-yellow tongues of flames tried to lick them as they ran.

Tara clasped her mother's hand, and, before fear could arrest her steps, they jumped. Flying embers singed her skin, her clothes, but she ignored it all. They had to escape the fire, alive. Or Layla would have won.

The back door was aflame. The bars on the kitchen window prevented them from escaping through it. Tara turned back to look at the way they'd come. A curtain of flames obscured the front room.

They were trapped. More bits of roof fell on them and Tara jumped out of the way just in time. Suraj was getting heavier by the second and Parvati was swaying on her feet. They were going to die in this inferno if they didn't get out within the next few minutes.

"Help!" Tara screamed. She stood below the window set high up in the wall and screamed once again. "SOMEONE HELP US!"

But there were no answering cries, no pattering of feet, and no sizzle of water, dousing the fire. Couldn't the neighbours see their house was burning down? A few seconds was all she needed to realize that no one was coming. It was up to her. If they died, Layla would be ecstatic!

And Tara was not about to make Layla happy. Or to let her win.

The kitchen was now hazy with smoke. Her eyes roved the room and stopped on the earthen pots of water. She galloped over to them and flung off the lids. She slid Suraj to the floor and emptied some water over him. Then she raced over to Parvati and flung some over her.

Parvati gasped as the water revived her.

"Mother, help me," said Tara. "Douse me with water."

Parvati picked up the pot and dumped the remaining water over Tara. The coolness on her skin after the fierce heat of the fire was almost too painful to bear. Tara scooped up Suraj again and moved toward the back door. The metal clasp securing it was red hot and there was no way she could touch it. They would have to force it open.

"As soon as I kick the door down, we're going to jump through, Mother," said Tara. "Okay?"

Parvati nodded, wiping the sweat and blood trickling down her face.

Tara approached the wall of fire, took a deep breath, and kicked hard. Her mojri caught fire, but the door did not open. She kicked the shoe off, sobbing with pain as embers scorched the sole of her unprotected foot.

"What do we do now, Mother?" wailed Tara. She was almost at the end of her strength. "We need something stronger."

Parvati pointed to the mortar and pestle by the door. "Use that."

Tara snatched it up. Sweat poured into her eyes, making it difficult to see. Her clothes were almost dry. If they didn't get out now, they'd go up in flames even if they did manage to jump through the door.

"Hang onto Suraj, Mother," said Tara.

She passed her brother over and then, using the long pestle as a battering ram, she charged at the door. The clasp broke and the door flew open. Cool air rushed in fanning the flames. They leaped higher.

"Now, Mother!" said Tara.

Holding hands, they raced through the doorway. Hot flames grabbed at Tara as she passed. They kept running until they reached the edge of the courtyard and collapsed, coughing and trembling. There was no crowd around them screaming, yelling, or helping to put out the fire.

It was then Tara realized; they were truly alone and utterly unwelcome in a place they had called home all their lives.

eleven

The Deadly Conch

A deliciously cool sensation woke Tara. She opened her eyes and stared into a face she knew so well, but for a moment her mind was completely blank as to the name and identity of the person.

"How are you feeling, Tara?" said the woman.

The moment she spoke, it all flooded back.

"I hurt all over, Gayatri-ma." Hurt did not come close to describing how she felt. It was as if someone had scrubbed every inch of her skin with a rock. Her hands and feet were particularly painful and burned every time she shifted. The stench of charred flesh lingered in the air, but she was so tired that she didn't even have the energy to retch. All she wanted to do was sleep for a very long time.

A sudden thought shot into her head. She struggled to sit up and realized she was on a makeshift bed in the kitchen. Gayatri was the only other person in the room with her.

"Suraj, Mother, where are they? Are they all right?"

"Relax, Tara," said Gayatri. "They're both fine and sleeping. Ananth managed to get the vaid to come here. He gave them both a sleeping draught so that the poultice can take effect."

"Vaid?" said Tara. She sat up higher, ignoring the dizziness. "So the villagers know?"

"Yes," said Gayatri. "Raka was here to take a look at all of you. He just left."

"I have to see Suraj and Mother, now," said Tara. "Please."

"They're in the front room," said Gayatri. "I'll let you see them for just a minute, but then you must promise to come back and rest."

Tara nodded and stood up on shaky feet. The kitchen see-sawed in front of her eyes. Gayatri put out a hand to steady her and slowly the room levelled out. Every step sent shooting pains up her spine. She could barely put any weight on her right foot. It was heavily bandaged and the bottom of her shalwar was singed and torn.

With Gayatri's help, she hobbled into the front room and stopped in the doorway. Parvati and Suraj lay on cots. The spotless white bandages stood out starkly against their filthy, soot-encrusted clothes.

Tara knelt by Suraj's bed first. He was asleep, but part of his face had raw burns that were still bleeding. He was dressed only in shorts. His torso was an angry red, weeping pus and blood. Tara wept, too, as she gazed at the little body. This must be so painful for Suraj. How long would it take to heal? How long before he would be all right again?

She kissed his forehead as gently as she could. Suraj moaned in his sleep, his hands clutching at the bedclothes.

Tara shuffled over to Parvati's bedside. She was asleep, too. The cut on her head was bandaged, a rose of blood blossoming in its centre. Her clothes were stained with red.

Someone in the village had played Holi with them, using their own blood instead of coloured powder.

Tara hobbled toward the kitchen, glancing at Suraj as she passed. He twitched convulsively, and then lay still. She couldn't bear to look at him anymore and returned to the kitchen as fast as her wobbly legs would carry her.

Tara collapsed on the bed and curled into a tight ball, fighting the urge to vomit. The villagers knew Shiv and Prabala were both away, so someone had decided to act now and rid Morni of its bad luck. She and her family had almost died. But who could have done this? Layla? Or had she put someone else up to it?

"Tara, eat this medicine." Ananth knelt beside her and held out a steel glass. Tiny white balls lay in the palm of his hand.

"Ananth! Did you see what they did?" said Tara. "They tried to kill us! While we were alone and helpless, they tried to get rid of us … the cowards!" Huge sobs shook her as she tried to get the words out. It hurt to speak, but it hurt even more to keep it bottled up inside.

Ananth's face twisted with pain. He set the glass down on the floor and hugged her. "I'm so very sorry about this, Tara. But you really need to rest now. We'll get to the bottom of this, I promise. But you must sleep. Take these pills. The vaid left them."

"No!" said Tara. "I need to talk to Rakaji now. I want an explanation. How could our hut catch fire? Why did no other hut burn down? Why didn't anyone come to help us? WHO DID THIS?"

"Shhhh, Tara. Just calm down and take this medicine. For my sake, please?" said Ananth holding his hand out again. "We'll … we'll figure it out together. Anyway, it's very early in the morning and everyone is still asleep."

Tara stared into Ananth's eyes, which were swimming with unshed tears. It was comforting to know he was feeling the pain, too. She was not *entirely* alone.

A strong and deep exhaustion pulled at her. All she wanted to do was sleep and the harder she fought it, the more tired she felt. She took the Ayurvedic pills and put them into her mouth. They dissolved on her tongue; sweet with a hint of mint. She took a sip of water and lay down.

"Wake me up in an hour, Ananth. Have to talk to … Raka … morning."

She had no idea what he said because she was already asleep.

• • •

Flames crackled all around, reaching out for her with fiery fingers. She was going to burn to death. Tara screamed and sat up, every part of her sobbing with pain.

Fire!" she croaked. "Help!"

"It's okay, Tara. Oh, my poor child," said Gayatri as she rushed over with arms wide open. "It's all right. It's only the cooking fire."

Tara came fully awake and realized that it was indeed as Gayatri-ma had described; a fire leaped under a bubbling pot of rice on the raised earthen platform. The house wasn't burning down.

"S-sorry," whispered Tara. She wiped her face with her sleeve. "I thought …"

"I know what you thought, Tara. I'm sorry for keeping you in the kitchen. But there is no more space in the front room. I'm afraid you'll have to sleep here and so will I."

Tara looked around and saw one more mattress rolled up in the corner. "Where's Ananth?"

"He's gone to get water; with five of us here, we're constantly running out. He'll be here any moment now."

Tara nodded. Her head was a lot clearer now that she'd slept, though her body still ached. She glanced at the kitchen window. "Almost morning," she said stifling a yawn. "How long did I sleep?"

"Actually it's evening," said Gayatri. "You've slept the day away."

"Oh no! Why didn't you wake me? I must speak with Rakaji."

"Not today, you won't," said Gayatri with surprising firmness. Her eyes held a hint of steel. It was the first time that Tara had seen this side of her.

"How are Mother and Suraj?" she asked.

"They're fine. I checked on them just before I started dinner and they were sleeping peacefully. But you can go wake them now so we can all eat something. Then you must sleep again. It's the best cure."

Tara walked into the front room as fast as her burned foot would allow her. Parvati was sitting up on the cot holding her head in her hands.

"Mother, are you okay?" said Tara, sitting beside her.

Parvati's head jerked up. She flung her arms around Tara and hugged her tight. "Thank God you're all right."

Tara hugged her back, an aching lump in her throat. Parvati's saree reeked of smoke, reminding her of their ordeal just a few hours ago. She took shallow breaths, trying to forget the ghastly night.

"Mother?" said Suraj.

They both rushed to his side.

"What is it, Suraj?" said Parvati.

"Everything hurts." He started sobbing quietly and it broke Tara's heart to watch him.

"You'll be all right, little brother. Just sleep," said Tara. She caressed his forehead gently and crooned in his ear until his restless tossing and turning subsided.

"Dinner's ready." Gayatri stood in the doorway holding a lantern aloft. The white of her saree glowed in the soft, yellow light, giving her a ghostly appearance.

Tara shook her head. She was so full of anger and hate; there was no room for food.

"Tara, you have to eat and get strong," said Gayatri. "Starving is not going to solve anything. Come along now, I don't want to hear another word from you. Let Suraj sleep. When he's awake, I'll bring him some food.

Again Tara marvelled at the steel in her voice. Gayatri-ma appeared meek to the world, but in her home she was a woman with an iron will. Tara sat on the kitchen floor, trying not to look at the flames embracing the bottom of the blackened cooking pot.

Ananth walked in through the back door, dripping with sweat, but triumphantly bearing two pots of water. "Had to walk to two wells to get these," he said in a tired voice. "But we should be all right until tomorrow."

"Sit, Ananth. Dinner is ready," said his mother.

Ananth settled down and attacked his meal with gusto.

"Thank you, Gayatri," said Parvati after a while. "My family and I owe you a lot." They were seated in the kitchen eating a simple dinner of yellow dal, rice, and boiled spinach.

"Anyone would have done ..." Gayatri replied and stopped. She took a bite of food and chewed it carefully.

Tara knew why she hadn't finished the sentence. No one had taken them in and not a single villager had stopped by to talk to them, either. Except for Rakaji, who had dropped in while they had been asleep. They were outcasts, just like Gayatri-ma. The thought made her chest burn.

Her mother still wore the blood-stained saree since the only ones Gayatri had were white. She had heard her apologize to Parvati for not lending her one; it was bad luck for a married woman to wear white.

Don't cry, don't cry, Tara chanted silently as she pushed the food around on her plate. How could things have gone so badly wrong for them? A few days ago they were the pride of Morni and today they were pariahs.

Ananth was quiet, too. A lot of thinking was going on behind those dark, black eyes, which seemed to be avoiding hers a lot lately. How she wished she could take him aside and discuss everything. Within her, one thought burned bright and strong; revenge. Kali was beyond reach, but she would see to it that Layla suffered. A lot!

"I need to go back and get some clothes," said Parvati. "I have to get out of these filthy ones. My skin is crawling."

Ananth and Gayatri exchanged glances.

"What?" asked Tara. "Why are you looking at each other like that?"

"I'll send Ananth to one of the villagers to lend you a saree and blouse," said Gayatri. "I know a couple of them who will still help us, though they might be afraid to do it openly."

"But why not our own?" asked Parvati, her face pale.

"There's nothing left," said Ananth, his expression grim. "Not a stick of furniture or clothing. Everything that could burn has gone up in flames. Only the pots and pans are left."

"Bela?" said Tara so suddenly that she almost choked on the morsel of food she was swallowing. "Did anyone get Bela out?"

Gayatri bit her lip. Ananth shook his head. Parvati's face crumpled and Tara could not contain her tears any longer. Their cow was a part of their family, sharing good times and bad with them.

"The shed caught fire too," said Ananth, softly. "No one could save her."

"Oh, Lord Ganesh," Parvati finally whispered. She dabbed at her eyes. "So we did lose a member of the family. Bela came to our house when I was married and now she's gone ..."

Tara stared at her plate, feeling like she had eaten too much. The food in her stomach threatened to climb back up. She was about to push her plate away when she caught her mother's eye. Parvati shook her head imperceptibly. Tara understood; she could not waste this food. It was from Gayatri's meagre supplies and it would be a sin and an insult to waste it.

"Eat up everyone," said Gayatri. "I'll make us some tea afterwards."

Night had fallen by the time they sat out in the

courtyard with cups of sweet, milky tea.

"Did Rakaji say anything about the fire?" said Tara without preamble. "Did he investigate how it started? Who's responsible?"

"No," replied Ananth. "He said he was going to call a meeting of the Panchayat to look into this as soon as he could."

"When is that going to be?" said Tara. "I have to be there."

Ananth shrugged. "I don't know." He sipped his tea, staring into the distance.

Tara wanted to shake him up. How could he be so calm when she'd almost died? They were homeless now and when Father came back, they would have to rebuild their hut. Too much was happening all at once and her head reeled.

"I must be there, too," said Parvati. "The fire was no accident. All this nonsense about us bringing bad luck to Morni has gone far enough."

"The best thing for all of you is to rest up," said Gayatri. "When Shiv gets back he can deal with it. It's only a matter of a few days. Right?"

They fell silent again.

"We have to see our home," said Parvati. "Maybe we can camp there and start clearing up as soon as possible. We can't be a burden on you indefinitely."

"Please, Parvati, don't hurt me by saying that," said Gayatri. She reached out and clasped Parvati's hand. "You and your family can stay here as long as you like."

"Thank you, Gayatri. But … I have to see the condition of our hut, see the extent of the damage."

"Not tonight. Rest today and Ananth will come with you tomorrow."

Parvati nodded and gulped down the last of her tea. Tara lingered on, still sipping hers.

"You go on, Mother, I'll finish this and come in."

Gayatri helped Parvati to her feet. Her mother swayed on the spot for a moment, holding her head. A small moan escaped her lips and Tara knew the blow to her head from the beam must still be very painful. They went in, leaving her and Ananth outside.

"How bad is it?" said Tara. She looked straight into Ananth's eyes, ready to pounce on him if he gave the slightest indication of lying.

"As I said before, it's completely gutted," he replied, not meeting her eyes.

Tara's hand shook as she placed the glass of tea on the ground. She took a deep breath and looked up at the sky studded with stars. It was the same as the night before and the night before that. But her life had changed forever and it had taken but a few minutes. Yesterday at this time she had a home, a family, and Bela. Today she had her lost a member of her family, her home, and her peace of mind.

"Why?" she whispered. "What did I do wrong?"

"Tara, stop beating yourself up," said Ananth. His voice trembled slightly. "It could have happened to anyone. The drought has made a tinderbox of our village. Any of the huts could have been a victim of a stray ember. I'm sure it was an accident. I think you should let the Panchayat handle this."

"But *any* hut didn't catch fire. Mine did. Layla's behind this. I know it!"

"Don't be ridiculous," said Ananth. "She's not capable of setting fire to anyone's hut. How could she have done it? Do you think Rakaji would not notice if she walked out of the hut with a burning piece of wood?"

"She could have started the fire when everyone was asleep. You know that she's capable of it! She does most of her dirty work under the cover of darkness."

Ananth was quiet. The dim light from the guttering wick of the lamp illuminated his grim expression. His black eyes were like stones. "I still think it's an accident. You should put it out of your mind. Tomorrow we'll go to your place and see if there's anything we can salvage before your father gets back."

"Someone just tried to murder us and you're telling me to put it out of my mind and go to sleep? Are you mad, Ananth? What's gotten into you?"

"Shh! You'll have our mothers out here in a second. You always like to be dramatic, don't you?"

Tara glared at him. "Layla wanted to avenge her mother's death, but this time she's gone too far. I'm going to stop her, once and for all. I don't care what happens to me!"

"How?" said Ananth. "By setting fire to Rakaji's hut?"

"I don't know yet. That's what I have to figure out. Are you with me, Ananth?"

Ananth scratched at the earth with a twig, not looking at Tara.

Tara stared at him, willing him to meet her eyes, to tell her it would be all right, that he'd help her.

He said nothing.

The oppressive silence weighed down on her. If this was the way he wanted it, so be it. She wasn't going to beg for his help.

"I think I'll turn in now," she said with an exaggerated yawn. And then, without looking at Ananth, she walked back to the dark kitchen and lay down on her makeshift bed.

Tara stared at the dying embers, at the misshapen shadows draped on the walls, at the unfamiliar kitchen around her. The ugliness of the past few days seemed to have buried itself deep within her soul and she wondered if she would ever be able to rid herself of it. A dry wind swept into the kitchen through the open back door. The embers glowed red hot, refusing to die out.

Tara sat up. She could not give up now. The fight between the mongoose and cobra flashed through her mind. The mongoose had strength, but the snake was more agile and it had won.

Layla had gone overboard this time. Each time Tara had not retaliated Layla had done something worse. But *this*, this last incident had almost cost them their lives. But how could she stop her?

Kill her, said the little voice.

Tara shuddered. Yes, that would be the easiest and quickest solution. But could she live the rest of her life with a child's death on her conscience? She moaned softly as the answer came to her. She'd rather face her own death than kill yet again. Already the nightmares of Zarku's and Kali's deaths haunted her. To add Layla's to that would be unbearable.

Lord Yama had said he'd take her to the Underworld to see Kali. But would she agree to stop guiding her daughter down the wrong path? Kali had spent most of *her* life making Tara's life miserable. It would be foolish to think that she'd help her now. Whom could she turn to for help?

Zara. It seemed as if Zarku's mother was whispering in her ear again. Now *she* was a woman worth admiring; a mother who had helped Tara defeat her own son for the sake of doing the right thing. And when it was over, Zara had willingly followed her son into the chasm. She'd be the best person from whom Tara could seek advice.

Yes! That was the answer. She would have to go to the Underworld, find Zara and ask her for a way to stop Layla. Then her family would be safe.

Tara hugged herself, allowing a moment of self-pity. By doing this, everyone would be happy. Well, almost everyone. She wouldn't be around to enjoy it.

• • •

The creaks from the courtyard became less frequent. *Just a few more minutes*, she told herself as she tossed and turned waiting for Ananth to fall asleep. Then she would make a move.

Tara stared at the ceiling. She was in no danger of falling asleep. Anger and fear clawed and gnawed at her insides, keeping her wide awake. Was she doing the right thing? Would her plan work? How would she locate Zara in the Underworld? And what if she met Kali or Zarku instead? Would they still have the power to harm her?

The mournful howl of a stray dog pulled her out of the endless vortex of questions threatening to overwhelm her. It was time to go.

Tara crept out the back door and stood for a moment in the shadows, listening hard. Nothing stirred. She padded softly past Ananth and in a flash she was on the road running hard toward her hut. *It will be in bad shape, be prepared, be prepared*, she told herself.

But nothing could have prepared her for what she saw. For a moment she wasn't even sure she had come to the right place. Her mind saw the familiar outline of her home, but her eyes saw empty space, illuminated by a crescent moon that hung low in the sky.

The sight of her home in ruins was like a punch to her stomach. Only two walls remained standing. Tara walked up to the rubble, unable to stop the tears. A heap of charred wood and straw marked the spot where she had lived since her birth. Here and there she saw a flash of silver; the utensils were the only things that had escaped, though not without a thick coating of soot. No one had even been by to clean up.

Inside her, sadness hardened into a shard of pain that pierced her heart. It hurt so much that she couldn't breathe. She thought of Suraj and the haunted look in his eyes as he had tried to sip water using his bandaged hands. She thought of her mother's eyes, sunken into their sockets, as she tried to make sense of the senseless, and she remembered Bela's soft brown eyes as she stood patiently, listening to Tara's troubles when Parvati had disappeared.

Tara couldn't even begin to imagine the animal's pain and fear when she must have seen the fire drawing closer. Could not imagine her final moments when the flames must have reached and engulfed her.

An involuntary sob rattled up from her chest and burst out of her mouth. She vowed to destroy Layla so that there was not a trace of her evilness left on this earth. Even if it meant that she, Tara, would not survive.

Tara starting digging in earnest, looking for the remains of the cupboard where she had shoved the conch shell after her last meeting with Lord Yama. It had to be there. But what if someone had found the shell and taken it? She refused to think about that right now. If she did, she knew despair would overwhelm her.

She stepped over the rubble; stray objects her only guide to the layout of her destroyed home. The stone mortar in which they ground spices was an indication that she was in the kitchen. The wooden pestle she had used to break down the door was burned and gone.

This was impossible! How was she going to find the conch in this mess when she didn't even know where to start?

Use your heart not your head, whispered the soft voice from within. Tara retraced her steps until she reckoned she was standing in the main room. She closed her eyes and envisioned her home as it had once been; warm, cozy, and full of life. In front of her was the door that led to the kitchen. To her left were their cots. The cupboard was a couple of steps to the right. Keeping her eyes closed, she walked over to it and reached out. Her hands clutched thin air. Tara opened her eyes and starting digging through the pile of ash and debris. Her hands touched something thin and hard. She pulled it out. It was her mother's necklace. The one she had given Tara the night she had disappeared. The mirror was shattered and shards of glass were still embedded within the triangular pendant. Tara had not wanted to throw it away and now she slipped the blackened chain around her neck. The cold metal against her skin gave her a bit of courage and she dug furiously. She had to be gone before someone came by and saw her.

Please let me find the conch, Lord Ganesh, Tara prayed. *Please, I need it. I need it so very badly.*

A few moments later, Tara's hands closed over a small rock with ridged edges. She snatched it up and scraped off the soot. A pearly white surface shone through. She stood up, her back aching, her pulse racing, and wiped the conch hurriedly with the edge of her kurta until it was clean. She looked at the debris one last time, then slipped between the huts toward the edge of the forest.

At the treeline she turned to look back. A starved moon hung over the village of Morni. She gazed at the village that had once been home, knowing that she would be living on borrowed time when she next glimpsed it. Once she called Lord Yama there was no turning back. Bela's soft brown eyes swam into her mind. She'd lost one member of the family. She couldn't bear to lose another.

Tara raised the conch to her lips and blew into it.

twelve

The Underworld

This time Tara did not have long to wait. Within minutes Lord Yama was by her side.

"What is it this time, Tara?" he said, dismounting. Each time she saw him, his huge presence shocked her anew. The god of death was here in front of her because she had summoned him! The thought scared her and made her feel special, too.

She folded her hands and bowed her head. "I'm ready, Lord."

His thick black eyebrows became a straight line. "For what?" he asked.

"The Underworld. I need help. Layla set fire to our hut yesterday. We almost died! She will not rest till she has killed my entire family. I MUST find a way to stop her."

Lord Yama stared at her for a long moment. "Do you remember everything I said? Once you return from the Underworld, you'll have twenty-four hours before you must return forever. Believe me, Tara, revenge is not so sweet when you finally taste it. Mercy and forgiveness are a lot better. Are you absolutely sure there is no other way to stop Layla?"

Tara was silent for a moment. There was nothing she wanted more than to go back home to her mother, to Suraj, and wait for their father and grandfather to arrive. It struck her then; she had no home! It was destroyed. There was a lot Layla could do before her father returned and she didn't want to wait around to find out.

"I've made up my mind, Lord. The only other option is to take her life and I … I cannot do that … she's the same age as Suraj!"

Yama knelt so that his face was level with Tara's. "My dear Tara. Once again your courage and selflessness touch me deeply. God has given you an abundance of courage and a huge dollop of recklessness. It will be a pity that Morni will lose you while you are so young. Are you sure you don't want to live to be a grandmother? You have so much in store for you."

Tara gazed into Lord Yama's eyes. Though a fierce red, they still held gentleness. She knew he meant every word he had said.

"What about the rest of my family? Do we all have long lives ahead of us?"

Lord Yama dropped his gaze and Tara's heart lurched.

"Someone from my family will die young. That's

it, isn't it?" Of course he would know. "Is it Suraj? My mother? My father? WHO?"

"Tara, I am not allowed to tell you. You know better than to ask me that question." Lord Yama got to his feet, his eyes flashing. "Don't overstep your limits."

"How am I to live, knowing that I could have prevented the death of someone I love? If I get rid of Layla then my family will be safe."

"Ahhh, Tara. When it is time to meet me, no one can escape it, no matter what they do. Do you think Layla is the only danger to your family? There are so many things that can happen. You cannot stop living your life, or prevent them from living theirs, for fear of death. Instead, enjoy each day to the fullest so that when it's your time to go, you'll have happy memories to keep you company."

"Easy for you to say," said Tara. "You have no family. How would you know what it is like to lose someone?"

Yama's expression softened. "Tara, I have seen much loss. A mother losing a child, a child losing both her parents, a wife losing a husband. I know loss so well — it runs like poison in my blood. But enough talk. Time is passing and we must go before day breaks."

Tara's pulse raced. "How ... how do we go to the Underworld? Will you have to kill me ...?"

Lord Yama smiled. "No, child, I'm not going to kill you. Get onto the bull and we will ride to the Underworld. There you will have one day to seek advice from whomever you wish. But I must warn you, it's a barren, lonely place inhabited by souls who have sinned or are awaiting judgment before they are sent to another place."

"And then?"

"Then you come back here. You take care of Layla and meet me at this same spot twenty-four hours later. Since you haven't really died you will live the rest of your life there until your soul is reborn. That could be a very long time. Are you absolutely certain you are ready, Tara? Time passes very slowly when you are alone."

Tara struggled to remain strong. Behind her lay the safety of the village and her life. Ahead lay the Underworld and two days to live. But it would also mean the safety of her family. She couldn't bear it if one more person in her family was harmed because she'd done nothing to stop Layla.

"I've decided," said Tara. "I'm coming with you."

"Then let's go." Yama swung her up on the bull's neck and jumped on behind her. He clicked his tongue and the bull started trotting.

Tara clung to its hump hoping she wouldn't slide off. She craned her neck for a last glimpse of Morni, but Yama's large body blocked her view. Maybe it was for the best. Now was the time to look ahead, not back, or she'd lose her nerve. And yet, Tara could not stop the fear blossoming within her as the bull started to gallop.

Around her the forest grew danker and darker. Barely any light reached the floor. Branches scratched her cheek and thorny bushes scraped against her legs as the bull crashed through the undergrowth, stopping for nothing. The odour of decaying foliage, rotten meat, and wet earth filled her nose. Tara had never been this far into the forest and she struggled to still the panic flooding her.

Soon the ground started to slope downward. Tara remembered her walk through the forest to the underground cave with Zarku. The Underworld would be way below that. She clutched the bull's neck, trying to fight the claustrophobic feeling that had always plagued her. She was almost ready to leap off and run back the way they had come.

"Is-is it very far, Lord?"

"Yes. The less you say the better. These parts are best traversed in silence."

The bull raced along the black carpet of earth, his thundering footfalls muffled by dead leaves. Trees raced past in an unending, shadowy blur. It was like being in a long, black tunnel with no end. Unseen arms reached out to scratch her, grab her, blind her. It was too late to go back. Even if Lord Yama let her get off now, she had no hope of finding her way back home.

They were moving so fast, they had left the heat behind. The wind blowing on her face was cool and getting colder by the minute. Her teeth started chattering and she let go off the bull's hump momentarily so she could wrap her thin dupatta around her tightly. Large arms engulfed her and immediately she felt warmer. The god of death was warm-blooded! Somehow she had expected him to be as cold as … death.

"Thank you," she whispered.

"It's going to be a lot worse when we get there," he said softly. "Rest awhile, sleep if you can. You will need all your strength."

Tara must have dozed in the warm circle of the Lord's arms because when she awoke, she realized two things at once: they had stopped moving and it was freezing.

Yama slid off the bull. Numbing cold pierced Tara's exposed skin, as if a hundred needles were jabbing her all at once, especially into the cuts and burns from the fire. She gasped and jumped off, too, wrapping the dupatta even tighter, wishing she'd had the sense to carry a shawl.

Tara looked around her. So this was the Underworld and it was not at all what she'd imagined or heard about from Morni's storyteller, Sushila Mausi.

Instead of the heat Mausi had described, it was bitterly cold. There were no fires and no people. Just emptiness as far as she could see.

The dark night was a vast blue-black tarp stretched tight above her. And then there was the smell. Tara had never inhaled something as foul in her life. It made her throat ache and her eyes water. Lord Yama was watching her closely.

"Where is everyone …" Tara started to say. A frigid wind howled past, snatching her words and scattering them in the air. A burning smell lingered in its wake. Tara swallowed. "WHERE ..." she started to say, louder this time, and once again the wind whipped around her, freezing her face, her lips so that she could barely move them. She stared at Yama, panic fluttering in her chest.

He knelt and beckoned to her. "The only way you can speak in this place is to whisper in someone's ear. Shouting will not work. The wind won't allow it." Yama spoke directly in her ear and she felt his warm breath on her cheek. An icy tremor shook her.

The darkness remained unchanged. No moon or stars broke the monotony of the endless sky. A barren landscape stretched out as far as she could see with a few scraggly trees and large boulders dotting the horizon. Dead leaves blew around in the icy gusts of wind. Everything else was still.

"So how do I start looking for Zara and Kali?" she said. "They could be anywhere!" The wind howled between them, allowing not a single word to be heard.

Lord Yama shook his head and pointed to his ear.

"Help me, Lord," said Tara, leaning close now. "If I can't even call out to them, how will I find them? The Underworld is so huge. Twenty-four *days* won't be enough, let alone twenty-four hours!"

"I've already broken a rule by bringing you here, Tara. I cannot help you anymore. All I can say is that you must bring them to you. If you think hard and get it right, they will come to you."

"How?" said Tara. She wanted to scream, but had to content herself with a whisper. "I hate this place!"

"Goodbye, Tara. I will return at the same time tomorrow to take you back to Morni. Learn to accept this place and work with its rules. You'll be spending the rest of your life here."

Tara's frozen heart nearly stopped beating as she looked around her. This was where she was to spend the rest of her life? This desolate place where she couldn't even speak normally? What if she found no one and wandered around forever, all alone? Panic grabbed her by the throat and squeezed so hard that she could barely breathe. What had she gotten herself into?

Yama's expression was unfathomable. Was it sadness, pity, or annoyance she saw? She clutched at her dupatta and bit her lip hard so she wouldn't start sobbing in front of him. He'd always said she was brave, but at this moment she wanted to fling herself on the bull and beg him to take her back home.

His massive hand squeezed her shoulder. "Remember, you have something very precious the souls here crave. Bring them to you."

Tara was too cold and numb to reply. She watched him gallop away. Within moments he faded into the barren land that seemed to hover between dusk and night.

The tears fell then and froze on her cheeks. "HELP!" she screamed. "IS ANYONE HERE?"

The wind swept out of nowhere and devoured

her words. The silence remained undisturbed and unnaturally loud; an incessant buzzing in her ear that was starting to drive her mad. She ached to hear the sounds of the living, the murmur of voices, the shriek of kids, and the tinkling of bells as animals moved in the fields, tilling the earth. Even Kali's voice would be welcome right now.

How was she to bring the dead to her when she could not even call out? Tara wrapped her arms around her, took a deep breath, and started walking toward a huge shadow looming in the distance. After ten minutes of fast walking, the hill seemed almost the same distance away as when she had begun. Her legs ached, and the sweat cooled as quickly as it formed, chilling her to the bone. Her foot throbbed painfully.

The monotony and silence of her surroundings shook her to the very core. Tara wanted to scream, but knew it was of no use. She collapsed on the ground, buried her hands in her face and sobbed. Had Lord Yama tricked her? Led her to this godforsaken land and left her to die. What if he never came back? What if he did come back and she had still not accomplished her mission?

Slow down, calm down, Tara told herself. *She* was the one who had summoned Lord Yama. He had tried very hard to stop her, dissuade her, but she had insisted. She had to figure out what to do, or this trip would have been futile. If only she could unfreeze her brain, she'd be able to think. She needed something warm — a fire!

Why hadn't she thought of this before? If she could light a fire it would be seen for miles around and everyone would flock to her. That was it! That was what Lord Yama had meant.

Tara jumped to her feet, trying to shrug off the weight of loneliness that was trying to crush her. She began searching for wood, crawling on the ground on all fours. The coldness of the earth seeped into her hands and legs, making them almost useless. A few dead branches littered the ground and she gathered them eagerly as if they were diamonds. Just the thought of a fire warmed her. Even if no one came, she'd still have the fire to keep her company until Yama came back for her. *And then what?* the voice asked. *You have one day of respite and then you're back again.* She pushed the thought out of her mind, the effort similar to pushing a boulder uphill. If she allowed herself to think about it, she would give up before she'd begun. One hour at a time. That was all she would think of.

Tara gathered as many branches as she could and piled them up. But how to start the fire? There was nothing around but rocks and trees.

Rocks! She'd use them as flints. Her bones ached from kneeling on the frozen earth and her fingertips were blue with cold. She stuck them into her armpits as she scoured the ground.

If only she had some matches. They reminded her of Morni and her family. Every fibre of her being longed to be back there. Once again, she banished the thought from her mind. *Focus on the rocks. Build a fire and then it will be all right.*

She talked to herself as she continued searching. *There's so much I've done already and this is just one more task I must complete. I can do this, I can. I must.*

At the base of a gigantic boulder she found a couple of jagged rocks. She examined them. Would they work? There was only one way to find out.

Tara hurried back to the pile of sticks, knelt as close to the wood as she could, and struck the rocks against one another with frozen fingers. One of the rocks slipped out of her hands and fell to the ground with a thud.

Her fingers were so numb she couldn't feel them anymore. She blew on them, but it was no use. The malevolent wind had picked up and blew dead leaves and debris into her face. Tara picked up the rocks and struck them again. Nothing. Not even a ghost of a spark.

Ten minutes later she was no closer to lighting the fire than when she had started. The only change was that her hands were bruised and aching, turning bluer as each minute ticked past.

"I CAN'T DO THIS!" she screamed. "LORD YAMA, PLEASE COME BACK."

The words echoed within her head. The still air around her remained undisturbed. The silence settled more heavily, more comfortably, on her shoulders.

Tara took a deep breath, fighting hard to hold back the tears and deep panic. *I will not give up. I cannot give up. I must not give up.*

Once again, she picked up the rocks and struck them against one another with all of her strength. One of them whipped by the other and pierced the soft skin on the mound of her palm. She cried out in agony, but there was no one to hear her.

Tara dropped the rocks and stared at the blood welling out of the deep cut

Someone whispered her name.

thirteen

Old Friends

Tara glanced up. No one stood before her.

"Who's there?" she whispered, peering into the shadows around her. The wind cackled in her ear. She circled the large boulders. No one was there and there was no place else to hide. So who had whispered her name? Had she really heard it or was her mind playing tricks?

Frigid moments crawled by. No sound broke the deafening silence. She was alone in this barren land and yet, she knew she was not alone. There had to be many, many souls here. Where were they?

Tara knelt near the pile of dead wood. Once more she tried to light the fire, but no matter how hard she banged the stones together, no sparks flew out. She leaned against the boulders trying to stifle the sobs trapped in her heaving chest. A chill seeped into her bones making her wonder if she would ever be warm again.

Tara closed her eyes and tried hard to think of a roaring fire, hear the wood popping and feel the heat rising from it. She opened her eyes and stared at the pile of wood. Her imagination painted leaping flames over it. Red and gold and orange, they would light up the place for miles and draw all the dead souls to her.

A frosty gust of wind swept her breath away along with the image of the crackling fire. Tara shivered violently. If she didn't do something soon, she was going to die here long before Lord Yama returned.

The cut on her palm throbbed. She pinched the skin together. A drop of blood, plump and red, oozed out.

"Tara, I'm here …" someone whispered.

Tara jumped to her feet, sure she had heard a voice this time. It was a soft voice, a boy's, and she had the strangest feeling she had heard it before.

"Who is it?" She spoke so softly, she was almost mouthing the words. This time the wind did not swoop down. "Show yourself," said Tara again. "Please?"

At first there was nothing. Then a shadow appeared near the woodpile. As she watched, the shadow became more distinct. A young boy took a couple of steps toward her and stopped. Tara stared at him, her heart beating fast, her arms covered with goosebumps.

It was Rohan.

Tears slid down her cheeks, freezing instantly. Tara fell to her knees and reached out for him, too choked up to say a word. The last time she had seen him was in the forest, with bloodied clothes and the burn mark on his forehead. Dead. Seeing him again made her relive that terrible and painful moment. All of the guilt came flooding back.

"How are you, Rohan?"

Rohan gazed at her, heartbreaking sadness etched on his pale face. He was dressed in same torn and bloody clothes. The mark of Zarku was still on his forehead; a deep, dark smudge.

Tara could not believe that Rohan could be here, in the Underworld! "Where's everyone and what are *you* doing here?"

"Lord Yama brought me here. He said that I had to stay here for one year before he could take me to a better place. He said I had to pay for my sins from a past life. That's why this one was so short."

"What sins?" said Tara. "I don't understand — you're only a child." She stared at Rohan, who was becoming more transparent by the second. He was fading away.

"Don't go, Rohan," Tara almost screamed. She remembered just in time that yelling was futile. She whispered her plea. "Please, I need to find someone and fast. Will you help me?"

Rohan nodded and Tara could barely see it. He was now only a faint outline, the landscape clearly visible through him.

"Where are they? Can you take me to them? I'm looking for Zara."

"Call them as you called me." His voice was so faint that Tara had to lean closer.

"Call you? But I didn't call you … you just appeared. Don't you dare leave before you answer me … ROHAN!"

Too late. Rohan was gone. The wind laughed at her. Tara scrambled closer to the woodpile and waved her arms above it. Nothing but freezing air slipped through her arms. She scattered the wood, whispering Rohan's name. He was gone. She was alone again.

"No …" she whispered. "Come back. Please come back."

Buzzing silence greeted her.

Rohan said she'd called him. How had she done it? Lord Yama had said the same thing. What had she been doing when she'd heard Rohan call out her name?

Tara went back to the spot and focused on Rohan, then Zara, willing them to come to her. She tried to think of all the dead people she knew and suddenly Zarku popped into her mind. She squinched her eyes shut, trying to erase the image. *No, not him. Anyone but him.* He would be here, too, and if she thought of him, she might draw him to her. Would he try to kill her again? Could a dead person kill one who was living?

Tara hugged herself. Her palm throbbed. She gazed at it and gasped out loud as something unthinkable occurred to her. She was alive while the others were dead. She had squeezed the cut on her palm and that's when she'd heard Rohan's voice. The power to summon them was flowing within her.

Her own lifeblood.

Tara picked up the sharper of the two rocks which she had thrown aside. She held out her palm, hesitated for just a moment, then jabbed at the cut. Red-hot pain shot up her arm and she fought against a wave of blackness that engulfed her.

And there was Rohan, standing exactly where she had seen him last.

"Not enough," she whispered. "Not enough blood." She squeezed her palm, biting her lip to stop from crying out. Another few drops appeared. Rohan became a bit more visible.

"You'll need much more than that to call the adults," whispered Rohan.

"Wait," said Tara. "Don't go." She looked around for something sharp. All she saw were the rocks, which were too blunt for what she needed to do.

Rohan drew nearer, looking at her in a curious, detached way.

"Are there many other children?" asked Tara, just to keep him talking while she crawled around on all fours.

"Yes, quite a few. Some have been a here a very long time and will ignore everything and everyone. It's the ones who've come here very recently who still long for their lives back on earth. Those are the ones who will remember the smell of blood, of life, and come to you. Like me."

"All right," said Tara. "But don't go. I'm trying to find something sharper."

There was no reply. When she looked up, Rohan was gone again. Tara thumped her clenched fists on the ground. Time was running out and she was no closer to getting the advice she desperately needed. If she left here without meeting Zara or Kali, this trip would have been in vain. She would have given up her life for nothing! *Help me, Lord Ganesh. Just show me the way.* There was no answer. Did she really expect God to linger in this cold, dark place?

The wind screeched and screamed through the deserted landscape as if mocking her pathetic attempts to seek company. Tara curled up in a tight ball and wept.

Something cold slithered against her throat. Tara screamed and leaped up, scrabbling at her neck, trying to dislodge whatever it was before it bit her. Her hands touched metal and she exhaled shakily. It was the necklace her mother had given her, the one she had rescued from her burned home. Tara pulled it out and stared at the rubies and blue stones in near darkness. They didn't glint or wink this time, but stared up at her dully. Broken shards of mirror reflected the blue-black sky above her.

Tara smiled. The smile turned into a laugh. The laugh turned into a shriek. Trying hard *not* to be careful, she pulled out a sliver of glass from the pendant. It pierced her finger instantly and blood dripped out.

The air around her churned with whispers. Dark shapes materialized everywhere; children, men, and women. About twenty of them crowded her, sniffing. Sniffing at the blood trickling out of the cut on her finger.

If Tara had felt cold earlier, it was nothing compared to the chill that now enveloped her. She clambered up the smooth surface of the boulder. "Rohan! Where are you? Come to me."

Tara scanned the crowd for the little boy. He stood on the outskirts, looking at her sadly. "I'm right here, Didi. Now ask them what you need, quick, before they disappear."

"I'm looking for Zara or Kali," said Tara. She spoke softly and prayed that they would hear her. "They died very recently. Has anyone seen them? I need their help."

"Yes, I have, Tara," said a tired voice. It was no use telling him to speak up. Tara slid off the rock and plunged into the crowd. Blood still trickled from the gash. Cold bodies pressed against her as she passed, making her shiver.

"Where are you?" said Tara. "Can you take me to them?"

A boy detached himself from the crowd and her heart skipped a beat. It was Shakti; the villager who had been hypnotized by Zarku, but had died. At least he had turned back to his normal self instead of looking like a Vetala with the deep gash on his forehead, the translucent skin, and the legs turned backward at the ankles.

"I cannot tell you about Zara," said Shakti. But don't even think of calling Kali. She's so angry with you … she'll do you a lot of harm!"

The chill in Tara's heart grew. Was it possible? She tried to ignore the growing fear. Kali was dead and she was alive. But in this frozen world of eternal dusk where people could be summoned by blood, Tara was not sure what the rules were.

"I need some advice about her daughter, Layla. She's the only one who can help stop her."

"Kali will not help." said Shakti. He was close to Tara, so close that his fetid breath fanned her face. She tried not to shrink away. "You should not have come here."

Suddenly Shakti disappeared and so did the others. A wave of dizziness swept over Tara. She looked at her finger. The blood had congealed and the cut was closing up. She would have to slash it again.

Tara closed her eyes, a deep dread flooding her; would there be enough blood in her to spill until she was able to get the information she needed? Would it be worth it?

She slid to the ground with a thump, holding her head in her hands. Of all the ideas she'd ever had, this was the stupidest and the most dangerous of them all. The cold was burrowing deeper within her, nestling in her bones, in her heart. She'd almost forgotten what it was to be warm. Exhaustion tugged at her, telling her to close her eyes and sleep.

Tara closed her eyes. She heard the soft tinkling of a bell. She could not tell if it was real or imaginary. Pictures tumbled into her head; her mother in the blood-stained saree, Suraj's burned body, and Bela with her sweet face and soft brown eyes. And then came the one she hated the most; a smiling Layla.

Tara stood up, grasped the broken shard of glass, and before the horror of what she was about to do could stay her hand, she slashed her palm. Blood bubbled out of the deep cut and her eyes watered as pain set her hand on fire. She closed her eyes to stop the landscape from shifting and sliding around her.

Whispers swirled around her like dead leaves, but only one registered, making her heart work extra hard.

"Hello, Tara," said a familiar voice. "I've missed you."

— fourteen —

Zarku

Tara's eyes snapped open. Before her stood a smiling Zarku. He was back in his original form; the one she had seen when he had first arrived in Morni. His third eye pulsed on his forehead. Tara pressed herself against a boulder, her eyes darting left and right. Should she run? But where would she go? Time was running out and she needed answers. Her palm throbbed and her legs trembled. She wouldn't get very far before Zarku caught up with her.

"You ..." she breathed, trying to sound calm. "What do you want?"

"You!" said Zarku.

Tara shrank back and Zarku cackled with laughter. It was the expression on his face rather than the sound that told her he was really enjoying this.

"Don't worry, Tara. I'm joking."

Tara's eyes swept over others who had also appeared, but hung back. Even in death, people gave Zarku a wide berth.

"Where is Kali?" asked Tara. "The last time I saw you both, you were —"

"Shut up," said Zarku. "Don't remind me of that time. She knows you're here and what you want. But I'll tell you right now, it's futile. She hasn't forgotten the loving words you both exchanged just before you killed her."

Tara had known Kali would not be of much help. Not after she had stomped on her foot and pushed her into the chasm. Kali's shriek reverberated in her head once more, drowning out the whispers around her.

"Where is your mother, Zarku?" said Tara. "She's the one I really came to meet."

"Not here," said Zarku. He looked at her with an unfathomable expression. "She's gone to a place she should have gone to ages ago."

"WHAT?" said Tara. The howling wind swooped between them and Tara remembered. She took a step closer to Zarku, every nerve in her body tingling with the horror of being a hairbreadth away from the person who had tried to kill her not once, but twice. Any moment she expected him to choke the life out of her with his thin, bony hands.

"Please don't joke about this, Zarku. I need to speak to her. Now!"

"I'm not joking. My mother had a pure soul. She was here for a very short while before she went away."

Tara stared into his face, inches away from hers, and knew that he telling the truth. The last vestiges of hope fled. Zara was gone; Kali was intent only on revenge. Zarku had always hated her; she would be mad to expect any help from *him*. Whom could she turn to?

She stared at the pale, sad faces surrounding her. The bitter cold had frozen all laughter, all goodness within them, leaving nothing but a shell. And she had agreed to spend the rest of her life here. This trip had been an utter waste. She wanted to sob, but even her tears seemed to have turned to ice.

"Why are you looking for Zara?" asked Zarku.

"Because of Layla," said Tara, too tired to think straight. Her plan had unravelled completely and she was close to falling apart, too. "She's wreaking havoc in the village and she's targeting me. I have to stop her. Your mother helped me once and I thought …" Tara stopped and clapped her hand to her mouth. How could she tell Zarku he was dead because his mother had helped her? In his rage he was sure to harm her in some way. She looked around for an escape route.

"It's all right, Tara" said Zarku. "I know everything. Mother told me she helped you defeat me. She was doing it out of love."

Tara stared at him, aghast. "And you're not angry?"

169

"We spent some time together before she left. We talked and cleared up a lot of things. For that, I am in your debt."

It was so odd to hear Zarku say that. "So where is she now?" asked Tara.

"A more comfortable place where there are no sinners."

Sinners. Tara repeated the word softly to herself. She had never considered herself a sinner, and yet she had killed two people in one body. Did that count as one or two? All she'd been trying to do was save herself and her family from death. Did that count as a sin?

The crowd that had kept away was moving closer now, sniffing deeply, reaching out to touch her. She stepped back, nauseated by the smell emanating from their bodies; the odours of decay, despair, and death mingled together.

Zarku was still calm, showing no signs of attacking her. It had to be a trap. He would probably strike when she least expected it. She had to be vigilant. "So what do I do about Layla?" she asked. "How do I stop her?"

"Kill her," said Zarku. "It's the only way. Use the dagger I would have used to carve out *your* heart. It has tremendous power; the power of darkness."

"How — how did you know that we …"

"Oh come on, Tara. I'm dead, not dumb. Suraj took the knife when you were chasing Kali and me. He's got it now and you know about it, don't you?"

Tara nodded. "But I still don't know why he took it?"

"My mother," said Zarku. "She's sure to have told him."

Now that he mentioned it, it made sense. It could only have been Zara. Maybe she knew this would happen or maybe she had guessed it. Tara thanked her silently; once more, Zarku's mother had looked out for her and she yearned to hear that soft voice one last time.

"Keep the dagger with you and use it the first opportunity you get," said Zarku. "It's the only way, unless Layla dies a natural death, and we both know that's not going to happen."

"You mean kill her? Kill a child?"

"Don't act like the thought never crossed your mind. You're not that innocent."

Tara looked at her hands, smeared with her own blood. And when she returned to Morni, and did as Zarku had said, she would have Layla's blood on her hands, too. Could she live with that for eternity? Zarku was observing her shrewdly. "You have thought about it, no?"

Tara gave a small nod.

"So go ahead. Do it! What's stopping you?"

"I don't think killing is the answer to everything. There has to be another way. Maybe if you visited Layla somehow and made her stop this madness …"

Zarku laughed, but all she heard of it was a faint echo. Once again it was the scorn on his face that told her how much of a joke her suggestion was to him.

"Tara, Tara, Tara. How can I ever explain the fun of leading an evil life? The power is exhilarating, intoxicating, and now that Layla has had a taste of it, nothing will stop her. Nothing but death. I am living — no, DEAD — proof of it." Once again, he cackled with laughter and vanished.

"Zarku! Where are you? Don't go yet!" said Tara. She whirled round. The crowd behind her was gone, too.

With a deep sigh, Tara looked at her hand. Streaks of dried blood caked her palm. She tried to massage it, curl it into a fist, squeeze more blood out of it. Barely a drop or two appeared. Her vision blurred and she felt lightheaded. She sank to her knees and retched. Nothing came out; there was no food in her and very soon there wouldn't be any blood, either. The shard of mirror, stained bright red, lay at her feet.

Tara picked it up. Could she do it yet again? Let some more of her blood seep away? The cold gripped her heart tightly, as if it would never let go. She could barely feel her arms and legs. Had she ever been warm? What was warmth?

Don't do it, the voice inside her whispered. *You already have the information you need. If you lose any more blood you'll die here.* Tara's hand shook so hard that the shard slipped out of her cold fingers. The only information she had was that killing Layla was the only solution. That was not what she wanted to hear. There had to be another way. She picked up the mirror again.

Ignoring the small voice screaming inside her, she slashed the other palm. A rivulet of red appeared, and trickled to the ground.

Immediately the whispers returned. Tara raised her head slowly. Her heart skipped a beat.

Zarku had reappeared, but this time he had someone with him. Someone she had dreaded meeting.

fifteen

The Wrath of Kali

"You touch a single hair on my daughter's head and you'll have me to contend with," Kali said by way of a greeting. She stood before Tara, wearing the same grimy saree in which she had plunged to her death. Her eyes glinted with madness.

"Then stop her," said Tara. Her heart thumped erratically, as if it weren't sure whether to keep beating or just give up. She wanted to stay alert, but the deep cold and her lifeblood draining away was making it impossible. She curled her hands into fists. The pain revived her. "I don't want to kill her, but if she goes on like this, I'll have no choice."

"What I was unable to finish, my daughter will. I'm very proud of her."

Tara glared at Kali wordlessly; it was hopeless, utterly hopeless. If the very person who could stop Layla was goading her on, there was no point in talking to her. Tara's eyes shifted to Zarku, who stood there quietly, listening to them.

"There is one other way," said Kali. "And really, it's so simple you'd be surprised."

"What's that?"

"She's only trying to avenge my death," said Kali, her eyes boring into Tara's.

Tara knew then what she was going to say.

"Stay back here and she'll stop," said Kali. She smiled, reminding Tara of Zarku's hyenas.

"Never," said Tara. "What is the guarantee that if I stay back here she'll stop harming others? She's tried to kill me and my family once already."

"You'll just have to take my word for it," said Kali. "But she'll stop."

Zarku burst out laughing. "Now I know why I used to like you, Kali. You're such a liar, you put *me* to shame."

"You both think this is a joke?" said Tara. She tried hard not to scream. "There are lives at stake and you're standing here complimenting each other? I should never have come. I should have asked Ananth to help me. We would have come up with a much better plan to stop Layla."

Kali and Zarku exchanged a look and burst out laughing. The sound barely reached her and for once she was glad. Their cackles would have driven her mad. Tara wanted to smack their laughing faces, but she restrained herself. It was wiser to conserve her energy.

"What's so funny?" she asked, looking from one to the other.

"Ananth, would have helped," said Zarku, wiping tears of laughter from his eyes. "*Ananth*?"

His third eye fluttered. Tara's stomach dropped. Would his terrible eye have the same powers here, too? If it opened wide would she burn to death? At least she'd be warm for a few brief seconds and then it would be over. She wouldn't have to deal with Layla or anyone else. But the eye remained closed.

"Would one of you like to share the joke?" said Tara icily.

"We're dead, but we still know what's going on in the world, Tara, especially Morni. After all, it was the place of my defeat. I'm not likely to forget about it in a hurry."

"Good for you," said Tara. "As long as you never come back, you can spy on us to your heart's content."

"Layla did not set fire to your hut," said Zarku. He watched her carefully. "She's guilty of a lot of things, but not that."

Tara stared at him. Was he lying? But why would he? He had nothing to gain by defending Layla. "You're lying to me."

Zarku shrugged. "I'm not, but you don't have to believe me. I don't care one way or the other."

"Then who did it?" asked Tara.

"Should we tell her?" Zarku asked Kali.

Kali smiled. "And spoil the surprise? No, we couldn't. That would be too cruel of us."

"Your trip here was a waste, Tara," said Zarku. "The incident that prompted you to come here was not Layla's doing."

White-hot anger replaced the cold within her. "The fire!" she whispered. "You mean it's someone back at the village? Someone else wants us dead?"

"You were always a smart girl," said Zarku. "That's what I admired the most about you."

"No!" said Tara. "That can't be."

"You have more enemies than you think. Especially with all that's happened in the last few days. Am I right, Kali?" said Zarku.

The flesh on Kali's face jiggled as she nodded vigorously, flashing a yellow-toothed smile.

"You're lying!" said Tara. "You both are. No one in the village hates us enough to set fire to our hut. They think I did all those things Layla framed me for, and they're angry, but not enough to kill … *not enough to kill me and my family.*"

"Believe what you must," said Zarku. He folded his arms across his chest and watched her.

Tara sat down with a thump, her legs unable to hold her up anymore. *Who* could have done this? Was Zarku lying to her? She looked up at them. They were becoming lighter, fading away once more. She examined the cuts on her palms; the blood had almost congealed. The mirror lay at her feet, reflecting the unchanging slab of sky. Tara closed her eyes, unable to cut herself yet again. She couldn't bear to listen to anyone right now, especially Zarku and Kali.

"You're on your own, Tara! And you alone must decide what's right."

Tara's eyes flew open. Zarku's face was a hairbreadth away from hers. His white-less eyes glittered in his pale face, reminding her of a cobra eyeing its meal.

"Trust no one. As for Layla; just wrap your hands around her neck and squeeze hard. It will only take a few seconds and then it'll be over. Or if you can find the dagger in the ruins of your home, use that. It will be much more effective." He whispered in her ear, yet she was sure Kali had heard every word.

"Listen to him, Tara, and you'll regret it," said Kali, leaning closer, too. Tara's nose filled with the unholy stench of death and she could barely breathe. "And when you return, you'll have to deal with me. I can assure you, the time I was your stepmother will seem like a holiday compared to what I'll put you through. And guess who'll also be here to help me?"

Tara squeezed her eyes shut, unable to meet Kali's or Zarku's venomous looks. Part of her still reeled with the shock of hearing that she had more enemies back home. But who could it be she asked herself over and over again. Was it one person or a few? Tara held her aching head in her hands.

A face flashed through her mind momentarily and she shook her head to rid herself of the image. It had been of Ananth. *Don't be silly*, she told herself. She was exhausted and her mind was playing tricks on her. There was no way he could be involved. But then who?

"You better hurry home, Tara. Thanks to my brilliant daughter, things are starting to get very interesting back there," whispered Kali.

Tara's eyes snapped open again. "What do you mean by that? What's happened now?"

But they were gone. Every last one of them. The landscape was desolate.

Tara was all alone with her thoughts.

sixteen

Twenty-Four Hours to Live

"You have twenty-four hours, Tara," said Lord Yama. "Just remember, whatever you do, you'll have to live with the decision forever, no matter where you are. So think before you act."

Tara was back at the edge of the forest. For a moment, she revelled in the warmth of the summer night and the sweat that formed a slick sheen on her skin. Never again would she complain about the heat. It had seeped all the way into her bones, thawing the agonizing chill. She felt alive again and able to think.

Standing at the edge of the forest, she could see that most of Morni was awake. Instead of the shadows and silence that normally cloaked the village at this hour of night, lights shone in windows. The forest seemed subdued; the stillness broken by an occasional chirp of a cricket or the mournful hoot of an owl.

"I must go," said Tara. "Mother will be so worried that I've disappeared for a whole day without telling her."

"That will be the least of your worries," said Yama. He looked at her gravely and shook his head. "Why must one so young bear such a heavy burden?" He said this last bit softly, as if he were talking to himself.

"What do you mean, Lord?"

"Nothing, Tara. But remember, you can tell no one about today — that I took you to the Underworld and allowed you to return. It's against the rules and would cause a huge uproar, here on earth and in the heavens. You understand? *Tell no one!*"

Tara nodded. No one would believe her, anyway, and if they did, another superstition would plague her — that she'd visited Death and would cause even more bad luck to befall Morni.

"Lord Yama?"

"Yes."

"Zarku gave me some information and so did Kali. But there's so much to do, I don't even know where to start. Please, can you give me two more days?"

"No, Tara. As per the rules, I should not have let you return. But you have shown such courage and selflessness, rare qualities in adults, let alone children that I decided to make an exception in your case. Don't ask for a second more. You can't have it."

Tara gazed at the forbidding face that had once terrified her. Yama's expression was still scary, but his eyes gave him away. Even though he was the Lord of Death, feared and reviled by all, he had a heart and it wasn't made of stone.

"Yes, Lord. And ... thank you."

Yama mounted his bull. "I'll see you here at the same time tomorrow night. Do not keep me waiting and don't make me come looking for you. Oh and one last thing ..." He held out his hand. "I'll need the conch back."

Tara stared at him for a moment. Then she slipped her hand into her pocket and drew out the pearly-white conch. The moonlight gave it a silvery luminescence. Tara clutched it tight. "Can't I keep it, Lord? I promise not to summon you again. I-I like having it with me."

"No, it's time you returned it."

Tara extended her hand very slowly, clutching the shell tight. Every muscle in her body rebelled against giving it back. Yama loosened her fingers, took the conch, and tucked it away into the folds of his dhoti. Stricken, Tara watched him.

"Tara, don't look at me this way," said Yama. His voice was gentle. "You don't need this conch. You don't need anything or anybody. What you need to defeat Layla, you already have. You trusted yourself once and succeeded. Can you remember how to believe in your abilities once again?"

Tara could only stare at him, a maelstrom of emotions raging inside her. With a brief nod, Yama turned the bull toward the forest. For a moment she watched him go. The countdown had begun and fear paralyzed her. She could not move, she could not breathe. Twenty-four hours and so much to do.

She looked at Morni, knowing it would be for the last time. She gazed at the Shivalik Hills surrounding the village, shrouded in darkness. *No time to smell the night flowers*, the ever-present little voice said. *Time to move.*

First she had to check on Suraj and her mother. Then she'd take care of Layla.

Tara sprinted to Ananth's hut, keeping to the shadows. Once again, the number of lit windows surprised her. Why were so many villagers awake? Low voices reached her as she sped past huts. Children bawled and mothers hushed them. Heat smothered the village and Tara longed for a cup of cold water. She arrived at the rickety back door of the courtyard, gasping for breath. The door creaked as she pushed it open.

"Who's there?" someone whispered.

Tara remembered that Ananth normally slept outside. "It's me, Tara. Er … go back to sleep."

Ananth sat up immediately, staring at her as she approached. "Tara! Where were you all day? And why are you creeping around in the middle of the night? Where did you go? We've all been looking for you. Your mother is out of her mind with worry …"

"I-I went for a long walk," said Tara. She perched at the edge of his cot, trying to catch her breath. "The fire and the situation with Layla was really bothering me and I needed to think."

"All day?" snapped Ananth. He stood up and started pacing. "You needed to go for a walk in this heat? You're hiding something, Tara, and you better tell me what it is. You're in a lot of trouble!"

Tara stared at him, her mouth dry. "What kind of trouble? Has something else happened? How is Suraj?"

Ananth shook his head and Tara's heart spiralled down to her toes.

"He's in bad shape, Tara. And with the other incident that happened today, the vaid has refused to come and treat him."

Tara didn't wait to hear any more. She jumped to her feet and raced through the kitchen to the front room. Suraj tossed and turned on his cot, muttering unintelligibly. Parvati was fanning him with a reed mat.

Tara knelt by his bedside. Seeing her younger brother this way made the room spin momentarily. His face was pale. The burns had worsened and oozed yellow pus and blood. He lay there looking frailer than she had ever seen him. Tara's skin crawled. He must be in so much pain!

Tara touched his forehead and jerked her hand back. He was burning up. The stink of blood in the small room was so overpowering, she almost retched.

"How long has he been this way, Mother?"

"Where have you been all day?" asked Parvati, her voice thrumming with anger. "Do you have any idea what I went through today?"

"I'm sorry, Mother. I needed to be alone for a while and so I went for a long walk."

Parvati stared at her. The next moment Tara was on the floor, her cheek stinging with a slap. "Our house burned down, Suraj is very ill, Morni is going mad and you *went for a walk?*" Her mother's voice climbed higher with each syllable and yet she was sobbing.

Tara flushed and the words almost stuck in her throat. "I just needed to think things out. I'm really sorry, Mother. It was a stupid of me. I won't do it again."

Suraj moaned and they both turned to him. In spite of the fierce heat, he was barely sweating. The fever seemed to have a very strong grip on him and showed no signs of breaking.

"Mother, you have to bathe him and bring the fever down. I'll get the vaid."

Parvati picked up the reed mat and started fanning Suraj again.

"Mother, he needs water, not air," said Tara, trying hard to keep her voice even. "What's wrong with you? Why are you still sitting here? We have to do something — quick."

"There's no water available, Tara," said a soft voice. Gayatri stood in the doorway, wiping her sweaty face and neck. "Not even to drink, let alone bathe in."

"Ananth didn't bring any?" snapped Tara. "Why? What was he doing all day?"

185

"Tara!" said Parvati. "Watch your mouth or I'll shut it for you. You will not speak in this tone to Gayatri or Ananth."

"I'm sorry, Mother. But at least Ananth could have brought water for us while I … I was away," she said. Both women were leaning forward, listening to her carefully.

"He couldn't because the well at Pinjaur has been shut down, too," said Gayatri, staring at Tara. "A dead dog was found in it this afternoon. The water is poisoned."

Tara felt as if she had just been struck by a bolt of lightning. She looked from Gayatri to her mother. "How did this happen? Don't they have guards at the well? *Who did it?*"

"Why don't you tell us?" snapped Parvati. "Maybe you saw something while you were taking a daylong walk." She glared at Tara, but her lower lip quivered. She bit down on it, her eyes swimming with tears.

"Mother, I didn't see … ohhhh …" Tara stopped as all the pieces of the conversation fit together. "You think *I* did it?"

"Where did you go for a walk in this heat? Did anyone see you? I know you're lying to me, Tara, so why don't you try telling the truth and then we'll figure out what to do next."

The room spun as the enormity of the words sunk in. If her own mother suspected her, then she didn't stand a chance with the villagers of Morni, or the Panchayat. They would tear her apart. Why, oh WHY had she promised Lord Yama she wouldn't say anything about their journey to the Underworld? She took a deep breath and looked into her mother's eyes, willing her to believe.

"Mother, do you really think I'm capable of something like this? Especially with everything that's already happened?"

"That's what we can't understand," said Gayatri. "It's just impossible. And yet … everyone believes that you're responsible for contaminating the well once again."

"There's more to this, isn't there?" said Tara. There was a sinking sensation in the pit of her stomach as she gazed at the two women.

"One of our large cooking pots was found abandoned near the well. It had our name on it. Since Suraj could not have gone for water …"

"But Mother, our house burned down! All our possessions are lying there in the open. Anyone could have taken the pot."

"Yes, but since you're already under suspicion, they all think it's you," said Parvati. "They think you're still possessed and that's why you're doing these crazy things, endangering the lives of everyone around you."

Tara opened her mouth, but no words came out. So this is what Kali had meant when she'd said that Layla had made things more interesting back home.

"Ananth told me that a villager of Pinjaur saw a girl throw something into the well and run off," said Gayatri. "It was in the middle of the afternoon and so hot that even the guard by the well was taking a break. The villager said he didn't get a good look at her face, but he remembers the clothes she wore. It was a parrot green shalwar-kurta with a yellow dupatta."

"*You* have a green shalwar-kurta, Tara," said Parvati "Everyone's seen it."

Tara clenched her hands. The cuts throbbed viciously, bringing tears to her eyes. She unclenched them, breathing hard, trying not to run screaming from the hut.

"Why would you even *think* I could do such a thing?" said Tara. "Because I like being thirsty? Because I want to walk even farther away to haul back a heavy pot of water? Or is it because I hate Morni so much that I want to make its people suffer? I didn't do it, Mother. Layla or someone else in this village is framing me. I have to get to the bottom of this. We have very little time."

"Rakaji was here earlier today, asking for you," said Parvati. She smoothed the wisps of hair that had escaped from her plait with shaking hands. "I said I didn't know where you were and he looked at me in a funny way. Tara, do you realize how bad this is? It's not safe for you out there. Gayatri, Ananth, and I are probably the only ones who believe you might be innocent."

"I know," said Tara. "But I have to get the vaid. Once I know Suraj is all right, I'll go and explain everything to Rakaji. He'll know I'm speaking the truth." She tried hard to smile, but it was impossible. She was tired and thirsty and so very scared that all she wanted to do was sit and bawl her eyes out.

"I think you should listen to your mother and stay here," said Ananth. "You're safer indoors. The villagers are in a very ugly mood. I'll take over whatever needs to be done outdoors."

Ananth had appeared so suddenly that Tara suspected he had been standing just outside, listening to both women berate her. Anger twisted her guts. Instead of helping her, he was siding with the adults.

"And let Suraj get worse? No!" said Tara. "If you wanted to help, you would have done it ages ago instead of waiting for me to return. You're useless!"

Ananth's eyes flashed and a vein throbbed in his temple. "You think you're smarter and braver than everyone, right? You always like to do things alone even when someone offers to help. Well, not this time, Tara. This time, you're in deep trouble and time is running out."

Spit flew out of his mouth as he spoke. Gayatri was desperately trying to shush him and pull him away, but he brushed off her hand and glared at Tara defiantly.

Anger and sadness filled Tara, making it difficult to breathe, or speak.

"You have no idea how right you are, Ananth," she finally managed to say. "My time *is* running out."

Hated and Alone

Tara stepped into the night. A searing wind swept down from the Shivaliks, creating dust devils around her. Visions of a tall glass of cool water taunted her and she clamped down on it before the image drove her mad. She had more important things to worry about.

She strode towards Prabala's hut, occupied by the vaid in his absence. She deliberately kept to the shadows, not keen on meeting anyone just yet.

The contamination of Pinjaur's well had to be Layla's handiwork. She had to be stopped and Tara had less than a day to do it. With a jolt, Tara remembered what had been bothering her ever since Gayatri had mentioned this latest incident. Layla had the same green outfit as Tara. She rarely wore it these days because Tara's had been stitched first, but she was sure Layla had worn it yesterday and destroyed it by now!

Tara seethed quietly. Layla could not have thought of this by herself. It had to be Kali. And there was no way to stop her except to kill her. Lost in thought, she hurried on, praying that the vaid would agree to come at this late hour.

"Try the well at Ramgarh and see if they'll let us have some water," a woman said. "I'm dying of thirst. What bad times we're going through; it seems as if Kalyug is upon us!"

"Enough, woman. Go back to sleep," the man replied. He stepped out of the hut and walked straight into Tara.

"Sorry," she said. "I didn't see you —"

"*You!*" the man said. "Don't you dare come any closer. I've had enough bad luck to last a hundred lifetimes."

Tara trembled with shock and anger when she realized it was Rohan's father who had yelled at her. When she had returned with Suraj and Sadia he had thanked her, weeping tears of gratitude and sorrow. Ananth had shown him the spot where they had buried his son's body so the animals wouldn't get at it and told him that it was Tara's idea. They had brought the body back and given their son a proper burial so that his soul wouldn't wander this earth eternally. Now would not be the time to tell him she had seen Rohan again.

"I'm sorry, Uncle," said Tara. She took a step back, hating herself for it. "But please don't say that. I've done nothing wrong!"

"Nothing wrong?" said Rohan's father. He spoke softly, but there was no mistaking the bitterness in his voice. "Your entire family is bad luck! My sweet Rohan was friends with your Suraj. Look what happened. Suraj survived and my son didn't. Oh no ... your type will always go unscathed while everyone around you will fall like dead flies. Get out of my way."

Tara stared at him, so shocked she was unable to think, let alone answer him. *Unscathed?* She wanted to wave her slashed palms in his face. She wanted to drag him to Ananth's hut to see Suraj's condition. She wanted to scream that she was so thirsty she was willing to drink tainted water just to quell the raging beast within her.

And she had less than a day to live.

But she said nothing.

Rohan's father spit on her. "Never show me your face again, Tara." He walked back into the house and slammed the door shut.

The saliva slid down Tara's face. She wiped it away with her sleeve, her throat tight, tears threatening to spill over. Rohan's father had been like a second father to her. He used to come over so often with his wife and little Rohan. He would keep them entertained with stories over dinner. And now he had spit in her face. If he, who knew her, could turn against her, what about the villagers who didn't know her well enough? How would they react when they saw her?

She finally understood the deadly seriousness of the situation and it was frightening. Going away with Lord Yama to the Underworld would not be such a bad thing after all. She had nothing to look forward to here but more insults and accusations unless the truth came out soon.

Tara stood outside the vaid's hut, staring at the dim glow of the lantern within. She walked up to the door and hesitated, surprised at herself. It had been a long time since anything had scared her, but the encounter with Rohan's father made her quail at facing another villager.

Should she come back with Ananth or perhaps Parvati? But there wasn't enough time, for her or for Suraj. His wan face flashed through her mind and stiffened her resolve. She knocked on the door sharply. After all, he wasn't just a normal villager; he was a healer and it was his duty to help the villagers in Prabala's absence. Surely he would be guided by his profession and not his superstitions!

"Who is it?" a woman called out.

Tara rapped again by way of answer, louder and sharper this time.

"*I'm coming*, don't break the door down," she said.

Footsteps approached. The door opened a tiny crack and the vaid's wife peered out, obscuring the light.

"Please can I talk to Vishnuji —"

The woman gasped aloud and slammed the door in Tara's face.

"No, please," yelled Tara. "Suraj is ill and I need Vishnuji to look at him right now. Suraj might …" Tara took a deep breath. She could not complete the sentence. It was too painful to think about, let alone speak out loud.

There was a low murmur from inside. Then silence.

Tara pummelled the door with her fists. "Open up! I'm not going until you come out."

"Go away, Tara," said the vaid. He must have been standing just behind the door because she heard him very clearly.

She stopped banging and listened hard.

"I'm not coming anywhere with you. Just leave me in peace and go!"

"Please, Vishnuji. Suraj's fever is very high and his burns are terrible. You need to come now … please …"

"Bathe him in clean, cold water," said the vaid. "That is, if you've spared any wells in the vicinity."

Tara heard the anger and bitterness in his voice. He had heard about the well at Pinjaur. The whole village must have.

"I didn't do it," said Tara. "But please, Suraj needs your help now. If our house hadn't burned down, my mother would have brewed the medicine."

She wanted to add that her mother made a much better potion than he ever could, but decided not to. She needed him right now and was willing to beg if it would help.

"God is punishing you for your sins," said the vaid in a stern voice. "Never thought that you would need water desperately when you threw those filthy animals in, did you? Now suffer along with the rest of us!"

"I didn't do it, Vishnuji. Why won't anyone believe me?"

The vaid did not answer her. The air turned hotter and stickier. Tara's clothes were plastered to her body and her skin prickled with heat. Just a few hours earlier she had been freezing to the core, sure she would never feel warm again and now she was burning up. She ignored it and pounded on the door once more.

"It's no use, Tara. I'm not going with you. I'll give you the herbs if you like. Boil them yourself and give him the brew. That's the best I can do. Don't ask for anything more."

"But what if he needs something for the burns, some salve, a poultice? You can't practise medicine from a distance. Do you want his death on your hands? What kind of a vaid are you?"

There. She'd said it aloud.

"The kind that would like to live out his life without being plagued by bad luck. Gayatri's presence in Morni was bad enough, but now you lot have joined her. Nothing will make me come to that house, Tara. I value my life. Layla warned me that ..." and he stopped. "Just go away and leave me and my family in peace. I beg you, Tara. Just go!

Tara sank to the ground. *Layla ... always Layla.* Everything came back to her stepsister. "Kill her," Zarku had said. "Just place your fingers around her neck and squeeze hard." Tara closed her eyes and tried to imagine it. Angry as she was, she still couldn't see herself squeezing the life out of Layla. But before she could think of her stepsister, she had to take care of Suraj.

"You're chosing to believe lies instead of saving my brother's life?" Tara screamed through the closed door. "You're a disgrace to the name of healers! I'll make you help us if it's the last thing I do!"

eighteen

Layla

Tara jogged to Raka's house, her anger keeping exhaustion at bay. Once more, she was careful to keep within the shadows, not wanting to face any more taunts or curses.

A strange feeling hung in the air, as if a thunderstorm were brewing. Tara prayed it would erupt and douse all the resentment and hatred of the villagers. The dark horizon was outlined in deep orange. Tara stared at it for a moment; was someone else's life going up in smoke? Their village should be slumbering right now and yet it seemed like sleep had vanished from this part of the world. All of Morni was awake and uneasy. It made her uneasy, too.

The sooner she got to Raka's house, the sooner she could insist that he ask Vishnuji to help Suraj. Then she could focus on why she was really here.

Tired, tired, tired, her mind chanted in time to the pounding of her feet on the parched earth. She reached the clearing in the centre of the village and collapsed on the parapet, gasping for breath. If only she could rest awhile and sleep.

A child wailed in the distance. Tara got to her feet wearily, aware that each heartbeat, each breath, was counting down the twenty-four hours she had left on earth. She couldn't waste a moment of it. She ran on.

Involuntarily, her feet slowed as they passed the spot where her home had once been. This time she took a good look. Someone had started to pile up the debris, but then abandoned the job. Soot coated the vessels that had once gleamed like a full moon in the night sky. They would all have to be scrubbed hard before they could be used again. Nothing else had survived; not a stick of furniture, nor a scrap of clothing. Even the medicinal herbs her mother had painstakingly gathered from the forest were all gone. They used to have such a huge supply that villagers were always dropping in for a potion for their ailments. And just when they needed the herbs desperately, they were gone.

And so was her home.

Tara stared at the empty space; one thing less to miss when she returned to the desolate Underworld. She didn't want to go. Her heart ached at the very thought. And yet a part of her realized that things had changed. Changed drastically and forever. Even if she cleared her name, she would always remember how badly Morni had treated her and the family because of their superstitious beliefs. If only her grandfather were here, things might have been very different.

Tara turned to go. A thought arrested her steps. There was something she had to do, something important. She squeezed her eyes shut focusing on the thought, which, like smoke, kept slipping away the harder she tried to grasp it.

She took a step and cried out. A shard of glass had poked right through the sole of her mojri and jogged her memory, too.

Tara yanked the shard out and ran through the rubble to the end of their courtyard. The pile of debris there was even larger. Tara dropped to her knees and started digging. The smell of burned wood and melted rubber assailed her nostrils, but she ignored it. She was looking for Zarku's dagger and this is where Suraj had kept it last.

Minutes flew past. Her hope diminished along with the dwindling pile. Tara's hands were black with soot and her fingernails were torn and bleeding, but there was no sign of the dagger. It was gone! At last she stopped. Someone might have seen it lying here and taken it. She wouldn't be able to use it on Layla. Her bare hands would have to do. But would they be enough?

Tara hurried on, resisting the urge to look back. She was thirsty, her foot throbbed, and the cuts on her palms burned with all the dirt and ash she'd dug through. She ignored it all, focusing only on Suraj.

Soon she stood outside Raka's hut. Golden light spilled out from the open window and lay in bars on the mud porch. She was not at all surprised. Tara almost expected to see a full Panchayat in session even though the hour was late. Good! If they were all here, she could tell them she was innocent. That Layla was to blame for everything; she and her miserable mother.

Tara stood in front of the door, once again hesitating to knock. Would Rakaji be fair as always or would superstition and pressure from the villagers cloud his judgment? She was about to find out.

Tara thumped on the door and waited. Footsteps approached. She shuffled her feet and said a prayer. Someone fumbled with the chain. The door opened and Layla filled the doorway, chomping on a laddoo.

Tara gaped at her. Layla did the same. Tara hadn't expected to see her stepsister up this late at night, stuffing her face. And from the look on Layla's face, she hadn't expected a late night visit from Tara, either.

For a moment Tara could do nothing but stare at the face that had haunted her every waking moment these past few days. If it hadn't been for Layla, Suraj would not be lying at home, delirious, while this evil child lived a life of luxury in the chief's house. Because of her, Vishnuji had refused to help them. The injustice of it made her want to choke Layla on the spot.

"Beggars should come to the back door," said Layla. "Sumathyji will give you leftovers if you ask nicely." She giggled at her own cleverness, bits of laddoo falling out of her mouth.

Something snapped inside Tara and she lunged at her stepsister. "You're the cause of all our troubles. You and your evil mother. Your mother is gone, and now it's your turn!"

Layla dropped the laddoo and ran into the kitchen, shrieking. "Help! Tara is attacking me. Rakaji, HELP!"

"Oh no, you don't!" said Tara. She raced after Lalya, grabbed her pigtail and yanked it hard. Layla's squeal of pain was music to her ears.

Raka and Sumathy who had been sipping tea in the kitchen, shot to their feet. "Stop!" said Raka.

Tara ignored him and chased Layla, who was now racing for the back door, dodging between Sumathy and Raka. Her large stepsister could certainly move when she had a mind to. Again and again Tara reached out to grab Layla, but it was as if she had bathed in grease. No sooner did Tara's hand close over a part of Layla's jiggling anatomy when she would wrench free and slip away, wailing loudly. Not a ghost of a tear appeared in her eyes, though. It was an art Layla had perfected at a very young age. It had got her and Suraj into loads of trouble with Kali. Now she was doing it again.

"Stop!" said Raka. His face was a thundercloud. "What is the meaning of this, Tara? How dare you barge into my house this late at night and attack your sister?"

"Stepsister," said Tara as she lunged for Layla, who ducked behind Sumathy. "She's made my life miserable, Rakaji. Don't you see that Kali has returned? Or have you become too blind and scared to recognize the truth which is right under your nose?"

Raka grabbed Tara's shoulders and shook her so hard she thought her head would snap off her neck. "STOP IT!" he yelled.

Tara stared into his eyes, which were like burning coals, and realized she'd gone too far. She had come here seeking help and yet had allowed herself to be carried away by the sight of Layla. Suraj and Parvati needed her right now and she had let them down!

All fight left Tara as she knelt at his feet. "I'm so very sorry, Rakaji. Forgive me. I-I ... shouldn't have said that. Please, I need your help."

Raka stepped back and looked at her as if she were a rabid dog. Layla stood by Sumathy, cowering and simpering. It was all Tara could do to stop from springing to her feet and slapping Layla for the show she was putting on.

Instead she closed her eyes and took a deep breath. *Focus, Tara. You need Vishnuji. Focus on that.*

"Sumathyji, I'm sorry," said Tara. "But I have a very good reason for coming here this late."

Sumathy gave her a scorching look. "Whatever you have to say you can tell Raka. I have no idea what's come over you, Tara. You were never like this. It's like … like you're possessed or something …" She shook her head. "I don't want to be part of this and I would prefer that you never spoke to me again. Ever." She walked away and Layla followed her like an obedient puppy.

As she watched Layla's large backside recede, she wondered why she had told Zarku she wouldn't be able to kill a child. At this moment she'd be able to throttle Layla without a second's hesitation.

Tara was alone in the kitchen with Raka. He crossed his hands on his chest and stared at her, not saying a word. In all the time that Tara had known him, not once had he looked this angry. Even the wrinkles on his face looked livid.

"I need your help, Rakaji," said Tara. She spoke softly, trying to sound respectful. "Suraj is very ill with a high fever and severe burns. Vaidji has refused to come and treat him. He needs help before it's too late."

Raka stared at her. The silence grew, filling the room.

"How can you just stand there, Rakaji?" said Tara. Anger simmered inside her and she had to work really hard so that it wouldn't spill over into her voice. "Have you managed to find the culprits who destroyed our home? Because of what they did, Suraj is fighting for his life!"

"I know about that," said Raka very slowly. "And we're investigating it." He did not sound enthusiastic about it, nor indignant, more like he was annoyed about the whole incident. Tara's anger bubbled closer to the surface. "But there are a few questions that I have for you. In a way, I'm glad you came here tonight."

Here it comes, thought Tara. She waited patiently, looking straight into the chief's eyes. She had done nothing wrong even though she had sworn to keep the last twenty-four hours a secret.

"Where were you all of today?"

"Walking by myself."

"Where did you go?"

"To the forest." The urge to look away was overpowering, but Tara forced herself to hold his piercing gaze. He had to believe her.

"Your house burned down, your brother is suffering from burns, and in this terrible heat you went for a walk, all alone. I did not expect such blatant lies from Prabala's granddaughter."

The words were like a slap. She had steeled herself for his anger, his taunts, but not this deep disgust and disappointment which marred his serene countenance.

"Rakaji, surely you, with all your wisdom, cannot believe that I am responsible for all the troubles in Morni; the failing rains, the dead animals! I did go for a walk and yes, it was a foolish thing to do at a time like this, but I needed a quiet place to think. You cannot punish me for being stupid."

Raka's expression softened slightly. "Tara, I don't know what to believe at the moment. I have known you and your family for a long time. There are so many things that are confusing, that are so out of character for you, and yet I cannot ignore the evidence in front of me. I have to discuss all of this with the Panchayat. We should be done in a couple of days and you will be the first to know our decision."

"I DON'T HAVE A COUPLE OF DAYS!"

Tara's hand flew to her mouth when she saw Raka's shocked expression. She was sure no one, least of all a child, had ever yelled at him. But why couldn't he see the truth which was so clear to her?

"How dare you raise your voice at me!" said Raka. His voice shook with anger.

"I'm sorry," said Tara. "I don't know what's gotten into me, but I'm just so worried about Suraj and everything else. You don't know the whole story, Rakaji. Time is running out and if Layla isn't stopped she could destroy us all. She said she'd make me suffer for the death of her mother and then she'd make the villagers suffer for throwing her mother out and —"

"Enough!" said Raka. He held up a hand. "I don't have time to listen to your ravings. I have more serious problems. The people of Pinjaur are very upset about their well. They shared the water with us and someone from Morni contaminated it. Their Panchayat is coming over first thing tomorrow morning to see that the culprit is severely punished and to decide what to do about the water situation. I'm afraid they might already have decided who that is."

"Let me talk to them," said Tara. "I'll explain that it couldn't have been me."

"Tara, you haven't even convinced *me*, how on earth are you going to convince a bunch of very angry villagers that you didn't do it? You didn't go for a walk and we both know it. Tell me the truth and there's a chance I could help you."

Tara's heart lurched as she met Raka's shrewd eyes, which seemed to look into her soul. She desperately wanted to tell him the truth. Later she would ask Lord Yama to forgive her. At least it would clear her name and everyone would stop hating her.

Tara remembered Lord Yama's stern expression, his last words: "*Tell no one!*"

Lord Yama had helped her when she needed him. Was it fair to break her promise just to save herself? What if the consequences of telling everyone that she had visited the Underworld were worse than keeping silent? What if it meant more deaths?

Tara clasped her mother's necklace, seeking comfort, a sign, anything. What should she do?

It was Raka who finally decided. "So be it, Tara. You had your chance." He walked out the door swiftly. "Stay here and don't go anywhere. It is as much for your safety as ours. You're just too dangerous to be running around the village by yourself."

"Where are you going?"

The door slammed in her face and the bolt shot

into place. She heard faint whispers in the front room. Then silence.

Tara pounded on the door with her fists. The cuts on her palms screamed with pain but she ignored it and continued banging. "Rakaji, let me out! Mother and Suraj are waiting for me. Please, you have the wrong person locked up!"

There was no sound. Where had he gone? Was she going to be locked up in the kitchen all night long? Couldn't he see that it was Layla who was a threat to them all! Tara paced the tiny room, wishing she had never come here. Mother had warned her not to go, Ananth had said the same thing, but she'd turned a deaf ear to both. The last few hours she had in Morni were slipping away. Tomorrow night Lord Yama would be back and she would have given up her life for nothing!

No! She was getting out. There was no punishment Raka could give her that would surpass what was already in store for her.

The back door! Tara had been pacing in front of it without realizing it was her escape route. She undid the chain with trembling hands and pushed the door open. Her heart leaped into her throat and then plummeted straight to her toes. Raka stood there holding a lantern. Behind him stood Layla. She was smiling, aware that only Tara could see her expression. The door slammed shut in her face once again. She was trapped!

"Let me out, Rakaji. I beg you. I have to go back to Mother. She's waiting for me."

Their footsteps receded. Tara raced to the barred window set high in the wall, stood below it, and yelled. Her throat was so dry and scratchy, it hurt to speak. The air in the small kitchen seemed to have evaporated and a massive headache pounded Tara's skull.

"Rakaji, Sumathyji? Don't leave me here. *Please*!"

There was no answer.

Tara ran over to a large aluminum container in the corner. It was so heavy, she couldn't pick it up. She put her shoulder to it and pushed the tin toward the window. Beads of sweat popped out on her forehead and her hands ached. When it was right under the window she jumped onto it just in time to see Raka stride out the courtyard.

"Come back!" she yelled, clutching the bars tightly. "Don't leave me here ... please ..."

Silence answered her desperate pleas.

nineteen

Trapped!

Wearily, Tara climbed down from the box and slumped against the wall, her face wet with sweat and tears. She'd tried so hard to rid Morni of Kali's evil legacy. But it had gone so very wrong. Suraj lay dying and not only had she failed to get Vishnuji, but she was doomed to spend her last few hours on earth locked up in Rakaji's kitchen while the real perpetrator was free.

Exhaustion made her limbs leaden. All she wanted was to sleep for a long, long time and forget about everything and everyone. But she couldn't. Suraj's burned face crept into her mind. Parvati's sad eyes haunted her. Tara got to her feet and paced the tiny kitchen. What must they be thinking? That she had gone for a walk yet again?

Unconsciously, Tara slipped her hand into her pocket. It closed over empty air. Lord Yama had probably known that she would call him yet again and taken the conch away. For a brief moment she hated him.

Tara leaned her head against the brick wall and took a deep breath. Why hadn't she just ignored Layla? Sooner or later she might have become tired of targeting Tara and left her alone. She beat her fist against the wall and a current of pain shot up her arm. She stared at the mutilated flesh of her palms; a stark reminder of what she'd been through and what was in store for her in a few short hours.

When she was gone, Layla was sure to destroy her family and then start on the people of Morni.

Why should you care? the small voice inside her said. *One of them set fire to your hut and almost killed you all.* This question plagued her worse than the thirst. If not Layla, then *who*? Who could hate her family so much? It was one more mystery she had to solve before Lord Yama took her away.

Silvery light illuminated the hot airless room. Its walls seemed to be moving inward, crushing her. Heat and thirst were driving her mad. Tara hobbled around the kitchen, peering into every earthen pot.

The one by the door gave off a delicious whiff of water. She sobbed with relief as she dipped a glass inside. There wasn't much, but enough to take the edge off her terrible thirst.

The water revived her slightly and she rested her forehead on the cool surface of the earthen pot, drinking in the fragrance of the wet mud. Like so many other things in her life, she had taken drinking water for granted. Only now that it was in such short supply, did she realize just how precious it was.

Minutes ticked by slowly. Tara thought of Parvati. Would she even see her mother again so she could tell her how much she loved her? Would she ever see Suraj running around, teasing her or begging her to solve a riddle? And her father? Would he return with Grandfather in time to put a stop to this madness?

A yell pierced the silence of the night. "They're here!"

Tara shot to her feet and stepped up on the tin by the window. The street just beyond the courtyard was dark from end to end and deserted. Who had just screamed? The street seemed to be breathing quietly, waiting.

Tara waited, too, with a terrible feeling that something was about to explode.

Pinpricks of light in the distance caught her eye. It looked as if a horde of fireflies was headed her way. Their intermittent glow disturbed the inky darkness of night. Then she heard the faint roar and her heartbeat accelerated as she realized what she was seeing: lit torches carried by a huge crowd of people, heading for Morni.

Tara remembered Raka's words. The villagers of Pinjaur were coming for a meeting in the morning. But it was evident that they hadn't waited....

The front door slammed open. Tara jumped down from the tin and ran to the door between the kitchen and the front room.

"Sumathy, Layla, come quick!" She heard Raka say. "We have to leave now!"

Where was Raka taking them? What about her? "I'm in here, Rakaji," she yelled. "Don't forget about me."

"Tara, be quiet. Don't attract attention to yourself in any way. And stay away from the window," Raka yelled. The door banged shut and there was silence once again.

Tara was paralyzed. Raka had taken his family away and left her here, locked up. Men were approaching the village with torches and they all thought she was guilty. For a moment the darkness seemed to smother her. She gasped for breath and dug her nails into her palms to stop the blackness from overpowering her.

"Let me out!" she screamed. "HELP!" Tara pounded on both doors in turns. There was no reply.

She leaped onto the tin. The glow was much clearer now and so was the smoke from the torches. Her skin prickled as she remembered the fire that had destroyed her home; the hot flames licking at the walls and reaching out for her with golden-tipped fingers. What if the men discovered she was here and set the hut on fire? There would be no escape. No one other than Raka even knew she was here. She would be burned alive!

The sounds of the mob were louder now. The yells were garbled. Then she caught one word, very clearly. *Tara.*

Another Loved One ... Lost!

The back door flew open. Tara screamed and flung herself backward, raising her arms to ward off an attack.

Parvati staggered in, carrying an unconscious Suraj. Raka stood by the door watching them. His turban was askew and rivulets of sweat dripped from his haggard face.

Tara ran to help her mother. Together they lay Suraj on the ground and made him comfortable. His face was pale and gaunt. Tara put a hand on his chest. Only when it rose and fell gently did she move away, exhaling noisily.

Parvati, too, looked close to collapse as she stared at Raka wordlessly.

"Mother, what's going on?" said Tara. "Why are you here?"

"Ask him," said Parvati jerking her head at Raka. She sank to the floor beside Suraj and sighed audibly.

With a brief nod, Raka stepped out and shut the door. Tara raced to it and pulled it open. "Rakaji, please tell me what's going on?" she said. "Is someone going to try and burn us up again? Once was not enough?" Huge sobs welled up within her, but she swallowed hard, staring into his eyes, silently demanding that he speak the truth.

Raka flinched and glanced furtively behind him. The street was still deserted. He stepped inside quickly and shut the door. Mopping his streaming face, he looked at Tara and Parvati.

"Tara, things are as bad as they can get. The villagers of Pinjaur are demanding blood — *your blood* — for contaminating their well. They're looking for you, but I told them your hut burned down and that you'd already left Morni to find Prabala. They don't believe me. They think you're somewhere in the village, hiding. The last place they'll look for you is in my house. That's why I locked you up and here you must stay. Don't try to escape. If anyone catches you …" He shook his head.

"But why do they want to kill me?" said Tara. "Surely contamination of a well does not deserve a death sentence?"

"Tara, there have been no rains. Crops are failing and already people are starving. They feel Morni's bad luck is spreading to the villages all around. They are here to take care of the source of it."

"Oh no …" whispered Parvati, her face ashen. "What do we do, Raka?"

"Parvati, you must do exactly as I say. I'm under a lot of pressure from the villagers to do something I don't want to. I'm afraid things are going to get worse. That's why I brought you here. And you must stay here until I tell you otherwise."

"If your house is so safe then why have you moved Sumathyji and Layla out of here?" said Tara.

Raka's eyes slid away. "I have to go."

Tara grabbed his sleeve. "Please let us go. We'll be safer in the forest. Staying here is too risky. If anyone found us …"

"No, Tara. The village is teeming with people. Many in Morni also think you're guilty. You haven't a hope of escaping unseen. Did anyone see you enter my house?"

"No," said Tara.

"Did you tell anyone where you were going?"

"Only Gayatri-ma and Ananth …"

"They won't tell anyone," said Parvati. "I'd trust them with my life."

Suraj moaned in his sleep.

"What about my brother?" said Tara. "He's ill and needs water and medicine desperately. You have to send the vaid to us now. Before … it's too … before he gets any worse." Her voice almost broke, but she caught herself in time. She had to be strong right now; there was still so much to do.

"I'm sorry, Tara. That will have to wait until this mess is over."

Before Tara could protest he had stepped out the door and locked it.

Tara hurried over to Suraj. A sickly sweet smell came off him in hot waves, making her nauseous. His fever still hadn't broken. She stared into his wan face and smoothed a wisp of damp hair from his forehead. Every fibre of her being longed to hear him say *Didi* once more, but he was deathly silent. Her fingers closed over his small, hot hand. She clasped it to her breast and prayed.

"Didi."

Tara's heart raced. "*Suraj*, how are you ... feeling?"

Suraj looked at her steadily with bright eyes. Too bright. He slipped his hand out of hers and fumbled in his pocket. It was only then Tara noticed the bulge. She pushed his hand aside gently and drew out a small package. It was heavy and without even opening it she knew exactly what it was.

"For ... you," whispered Suraj. He closed his eyes, breathing raggedly.

"What is it, Tara?" asked Parvati. "What's in the parcel?"

"Something he wants me to keep safe for him," said Tara. She gazed into Suraj's face, feeling as if her heart would burst with pain.

Parvati did not ask any more questions as Tara tucked the bundle into her pocket wondering when she would get a chance to use it.

Once again she took Suraj's hand and clasped it to her chest. *Stay strong Suraj, for my sake stay strong for just a little while longer.*

• • •

Minutes, which felt like days, crawled by. Flies attacked Suraj mercilessly. Parvati and Tara waved them away, but in a few moments they were back again, crawling over the exposed burns. Suraj twitched once or twice and then lay still, his laborious breathing filling the room.

"Mother, what's going to happen to us?"

"I don't know, Tara. We can only hope and pray that your grandfather reaches us in time. If only you hadn't gone off for a walk, things wouldn't have gotten out of hand. At a time like this couldn't you have thought about others rather than yourself?"

The words were like knives through Tara's heart. Her own mother thought she was being selfish! Going to the Underworld had been one of the most difficult decisions she'd had to make. And the most selfless. She wanted to scream at her mother to wipe the disappointment from her face because her daughter wasn't someone to be ashamed of! But Tara did not utter a word. A promise was a promise though the injustice of it all was burning her up inside.

"It's all because of Layla," Tara said finally. "Suraj and I warned you, Mother. We told you she was evil, just

217

like Kali. Maybe even more so, but you wouldn't listen. And now look at what the snake has done to us. She's bitten the hand that fed her."

"But, Tara, if you weren't there, how did someone see you walk away from the well?"

Tara sighed. "Mother don't you remember? Layla had sulked after I got the new green shalwar-kurta. So, with the remaining cloth you had the tailor stitch her one, too."

She watched Parvati's face as realization dawned. "Yes ... yes of course. I'd completely forgotten about it. You mean she deliberately framed you? But she's just a child ... are you sure?"

"YES!" said Tara. "That's what I've been trying to tell everyone! But no one will believe that a *child* can be so vengeful and clever, too. She's the cause of all this. She and her mother." It slipped out before Tara could stop herself.

"Kali?" said Parvati. "But Kali is dead. You said so yourself. How can Kali be responsible?"

"I-I meant she has the same blood as Kali. Right? Layla is finally showing her true colours."

Parvati shook her head. "I still can't believe a child could go to such lengths.... She's only nine."

"If she can do so much damage now," said Tara softly, "think of what she'll be capable of when she gets older."

Parvati opened her mouth. No words came out.

A deep voice outside the door shattered the silence. "Where's Tara? Has anyone seen her, or her family?"

Tara froze and clasped Suraj's hand tighter in hers. Parvati put a finger to her lips. She walked to the window, stood on the tin and peered out carefully. Tara watched her, tense as a tightly coiled spring. They were such an easy target in this place. Once the villagers knew where they were hidden, they were as good as dead.

A few moments later Parvati tiptoed back, her face paler than the whitewashed walls around her. Tara was afraid she was about to faint. She pulled her mother to the floor and slid closer, still holding on to Suraj. The three of them sat in silence, holding hands.

And yet Tara was acutely aware of a fourth unwelcome guest in the room — fear.

"They're searching for you," said Parvati softly. "But they've moved to the next hut. I pray they don't come back." Her voice trembled.

Tara took a deep breath, listening hard. The voices of the villagers became louder as they passed by the hut in the opposite direction and then died away. They were safe for now. Deep silence fell once more. Tara looked around the room; at her mother, at Suraj. Something was not quite right.

The truth crashed over her like a tidal wave.

She was still clutching Suraj's little hand, but he had slipped away from her grasp forever.

twenty-one

Time for Justice

Tara clutched Suraj's hand tighter, never wanting to let go.

"Let him sleep," said Parvati. "If he wakes, he'll ask for water."

Tara shook her head, trying hard to suppress a sob. The shadows, draped around the room seemed blacker than ever before, filling her with a deep dread. She wanted to lie down next to Suraj and never wake up.

She knelt beside her little brother. His eyes were closed, his face almost bloodless. Yet, there was a hint of a smile. As if he had been happy about something during his final moments. Tara choked back another sob and brushed his forehead with her lips. "I'm sorry," she whispered. "I'm so very, very sorry."

"For what, Tara?" said Parvati. 'You didn't hurt him."

"He's gone, Mother." Tara stuffed a knuckle into her

mouth to stop the scream that was building up inside her.

Parvati stared at her, uncomprehending, and then she looked at Suraj. She touched his skin and jerked her hand away. Tara knew why. His body, which had been burning just a short while ago, was cooling rapidly.

"No," said Parvati. "No, this cannot be."

She gathered Suraj in her arms and hugged him tight, sobbing softly. Tara moved closer. Her arm brushed a burn on Suraj's shoulder and instinctively she pulled away, expecting him to whimper. Then she realized he wouldn't make a sound. Ever again.

Flies buzzed around them, drawn by Suraj's wounds. The kitchen was a furnace and yet Tara was cold. As time passed, the cold hardened into anger. Then rage. She had lost her baby brother because of Layla. In spite of everything she had done to save him from Kali and then Zarku, she'd still lost him. To an evil *child*.

If Layla were in front of her right now, she wouldn't hesitate to squeeze her neck as slowly as possible, until Layla's eyes popped and she breathed her last.

Suddenly Tara couldn't sit still a moment longer. She jumped to her feet and grabbed the large, wooden pestle by the kitchen door.

"What are you doing?" said Parvati, her voice still weepy.

"Getting us out of here."

"Sit down. If the villagers hear you ..." She started sobbing again, clutching Suraj tighter.

Tara stared at her helplessly. She wanted to comfort her mother, but she also wanted to escape. The night was fading and she was nowhere close to accomplishing what she had set out to do.

"I'm tired of sitting and waiting," said Tara. "I have to do something or I'll go mad."

She held the long wooden pestle in front of her like a battering ram and charged at the door leading to the front room. The shock of the impact threw her backward. The door held. Tara shook out her aching arms. One of the cuts in her palm had opened up again and blood seeped through, but she didn't care. All she saw was a door that separated her from Layla and she had to break it down. Before her time ran out, her stepsister would be dead!

Tara walked farther back and once again charged the door. The pestle broke with a loud crack, showering her with splinters of wood. Her body thrummed with the impact, but the door barely had a dent in it. "Tara you'll hurt yourself," said Parvati. "I couldn't bear to lose you, too. Can you please just sit down?" Her mother's voice shook so much that Tara abandoned her attempt to escape and hugged her.

Parvati's chest heaved with silent sobs as she clung to her. By this time tomorrow she'd have lost both her children thought Tara. Would she be able to bear it? With her father and grandfather still away, whom would her mother turn to for solace? All of these thoughts tumbled around in Tara's head, numbing her with worry.

"It's all right, Mother," said Tara. "I'm here. I'm not going anywhere."

"Has anyone checked Raka's hut?" A gruff voice spoke just outside their door.

Parvati and Tara both stiffened. Tara suddenly realized that she could see her mother's tear-blotched face and red-rimmed eyes clearly. It was almost dawn. She looked at Suraj. The rigidness of his face was apparent now that the shroud of darkness had melted away. Tara wanted to weep anew. Parvati's gaze searched the room and Tara knew why. They couldn't leave Suraj like this.

Tara pulled off the bright yellow duppata from around her neck. She loved yellow. It was the colour of sunshine, the colour of life. She shook it out and covered Suraj's body, giving him some dignity in death.

"That's Raka's hut," another voice said. "Surely you don't think Tara …"

"Search every house no matter whose it is," said the first voice. "Those were Kripan's orders."

Footsteps stopped outside the back door. Tara and Parvati crouched in a corner as far away from the door as possible. The kitchen had no furniture. There was nowhere to hide.

"The door's locked from the outside. Now why would anyone lock a *kitchen* door from the outside?"

"Break it! Now!"

Tara's heart pounded in tandem with the blows on the lock. She clutched her mother's hand as they pressed themselves against the far wall. Within seconds the lock broke and fell to the ground with a dull thud. The door crashed open.

Parvati screamed as two villagers rushed into the room. One was a large brute and the other was short and stocky. Neither was from Morni.

"Found her, at last," said one, a triumphant note in his voice. "It's time to bring you to justice, Tara."

twenty-two

The Beginning of the End

"**N**o!" Parvati screamed. "You're not taking my daughter anywhere. You'll have to kill me first." She stepped in front of Tara, shielding her.

"Hand her over," the brute said. He was so large, he towered over them both. His swarthy complexion glistened with sweat in the early-morning light filtering into the kitchen.

"No!" said Parvati.

Both men advanced into the room.

"Look, woman, we don't want trouble. We have orders to bring Tara to the meeting organized by the Panchayats of Morni and Pinjaur. Let her come with us and no one will get hurt."

"*You* will get hurt if you lay a hand on her," said Parvati quietly. "Go away. Now!"

The men glanced at each other momentarily. "We'll

say this one last time. Step aside," said Shorty. "We'll carry Tara out of here if we have to."

"There's no need," said Tara. "I'll go with you."

"Tara, no," said her mother. She faced Tara and clasped her hands. "You can't do this. What if they find you guilty? I'll lose ..." Her lower lip quivered and she bit down hard on it.

"Oh, Mother." Tara hugged her tightly, trying to blink back tears. She desperately wanted to tell her mother that it was no use protecting her or holding her back. Her time was up at the end of the day. It made more sense to go with these people. If the Panchayat was meeting in front of all the villagers, Layla was sure to be there.

And that's all she wanted. To face Layla one last time, to look into her eyes, see the pain and fear on her face when she killed her. In spite of the queasiness, she couldn't wait to go with the men and get it over with. "Mother, I have to go, you stay here ... with Suraj."

"I can't let you go alone, Tara. I'm coming with you."

"You should listen to your daughter, woman," said the brute. "Stay here with your sleeping child. If she's innocent, we'll bring her back in no time at all."

"Shut up!" spluttered Parvati. "Don't you *dare* tell me what to do." In two strides she was beside Suraj. She flung Tara's dupatta off his body. Flies buzzed over her brother, crawled over his face, and into his mouth. His pale skin looked as if it were carved from stone.

226

Tara swayed on the spot and looked away, trying to control her heaving stomach and the tears that welled up in her eyes once again. He should not be dead. He *would* not have been dead if it hadn't been for the person who had torched their home and happiness. Layla was definitely involved. Anger sprang up within her like a hungry beast. Just before she squeezed the life out of Layla, she would squeeze out the name of the person who had killed her brother.

"This is my son, Suraj," said Parvati. "He's dead because he could not get help in time. Why don't *you* stay with him while I go make preparations for the funeral?"

"We're ... we're very sorry, Sister," said the burly man. His voice had softened. The other one looked ashamed, too. "We didn't realize that ... he was —"

"Dead. But now you do," said Parvati. "If you take Tara, this could be her fate. Do you want me to prepare for two funerals? If you were in my place, would you be able to hand over your second child right after losing the first?" She looked from one to the other. "ANSWER ME!"

"If she's innocent then you have nothing to worry about," the brute said. "All we're doing is taking her to a meeting." He said this very softly. It was evident that he didn't believe a word of it.

"Is it normal practice to invade a village in the middle of the night and hold a Panchayat because a well was contaminated? You lie to my face that my child might

227

be found innocent?" Parvati dabbed at the tears leaking from her eyes and it took all of Tara's self control not to break down, too.

"Mother, we both know I have to go," said Tara finally. Parvati was crying too hard to say another word. "Stay here with Suraj. I'll send word to Gayatri-ma or Ananth to help you. Trust me, Mother, it will be all right. I'm innocent and God will be by my side." Her voice wobbled dangerously as she said that. There would definitely be a god by her side: the god of death.

Parvati looked deep into her eyes and Tara had a bad feeling this might be the last time she would see her mother. She wanted to cling to her and never let go.

"You've always been my guiding star," said Parvati. "And since I came back to Morni, you've shone brighter than ever. May the blessings of Lord Ganesh be with you." Her mother kissed her forehead and stepped back.

Tara hurried to the door before she lost her nerve. The men followed her. She stepped over the threshold and looked back. Suraj's body was still uncovered. His small hand lay on his chest. Tara gazed at him for a long moment. Then she turned and walked out into the bright dawn of her last day in Morni.

twenty-three

Panchayats and Promises

The village centre thronging with people resembled a fair, almost like the one at Ambala. The memory of Suraj and Rohan resurfaced and pain clutched at her heart. If anyone had told her that within a few months both of these children would be dead she would have slapped that person.

Why hadn't she savoured the time with Suraj when she'd had the chance? Why hadn't she played with him more often, told him that she loved him? Now it was too late.

"Faster," said one of the men, poking her in the back. "We don't have all day."

Tara glared at him, deliberately slowing down. Hundreds of villagers were seated around the banyan tree. There was a buzz in the air, as if they were waiting for a performance to start. As she made her way to the front of the crowd, it dawned on her that she was the attraction. Today they would make her the scapegoat and punish her, hoping that the weather and their fortunes would improve. But they were so wrong. The person responsible for all of their troubles was still on the loose.

People hissed and booed as she walked past. Some villagers leaped out of the way, as if her very shadow would strike them dead. The sight of grown men acting so weird made her want to laugh out loud. But she was terrified, too. This mob looked angry enough for blood and a fair trial seemed impossible. She remembered Kali's trial and how incensed the villagers had been. Tara continued walking, her head held high, refusing to let fear overwhelm her.

The crowd was yelling. Most of it was just noise, but a few insults she heard clearly;

"Zarku's messenger."

"Evil witch."

"Fallen star."

"Brave Tara."

She tasted salt at the back of her throat and swallowed. There was at least one supporter in this mad crowd. She scanned the faces, hoping it was Ananth. But there was no sign of him or Gayatri.

And Layla. Where was she? Kali had worked so hard for this moment and it was impossible that Layla would stay away. Tara reached the front of the crowd and waited.

The members of the Panchayat were already seated on the platform. Raka and the other elders nodded at her. Next to Morni's elders sat the Panchayat of Pinjaur. Five pairs of hostile eyes bored into her. She met their gazes without flinching. She would not give them, or the crowd, the satisfaction of seeing just how petrified she was. The sun climbed higher into the sky, baking her head. Thirst clawed at her throat and fear gnawed her insides.

The noise swelled behind her, but she did not turn around. Instead, she gazed at the Panchayat, one at a time, willing them to believe she was innocent.

At long last, Raka held up his hand. Immediately, the villagers fell silent. He cleared his throat and spoke. "Tara, you are here because you have been charged with contaminating the well at Pinjaur and also defiling our temple. Morni's well was also contaminated, but we're still investigating it. What do you have to say for yourself?"

Tara stared at him. *They were actually giving her a chance to speak?* She held her head high and spoke. "Rakaji, I am not responsible for either of the two incidents."

Jeers rose from the crowd behind her. Though her pulse raced, she ignored them.

"We are not concerned about *your* village well," said Kripan, the head of Pinjaur's Panchayat. "All we want to know is how and why you contaminated *our* well when we were being neighbourly and allowing you to share our water? Why would you put so many lives at risk when you know the rains have failed and this is our only source of water? Are you mad or possessed?"

"Hold on, Kripan," said Raka. "We are here to *prove* she did it, not *assume* she's guilty."

"No adult could do something so harmful knowing he or she would suffer, too," Kripan snapped back. "This has to be the work of a misguided child ..."

"Or someone really evil," a voice shouted from the crowd. "Someone who has spent a lot of time with the devil himself."

Hatred coursed through Tara as she recognized the voice. She turned around and spotted Layla; a small, fat toad nestled between the villagers. Layla looked at her steadily, the corners of her mouth upturned.

"This is not yet open to discussion," said Raka, frowning at Layla. "When we ask for everyone's opinion, you may speak then."

Layla pouted, but no one paid attention.

"What was the result of your investigation regarding the dead animal in your temple, Raka?" asked Kripan. "Surely for something this serious you would have put all your efforts into it?" The contempt in his voice was unmistakable.

"We did and we're still working on it," said Raka. His voice was firm. "However, Tara has already paid for it, despite the fact that other than her dupatta, there is no further evidence to suggest she did it. There's no motive, either."

"And your own well?" said Kripan. "How did the dead cat get in there? You keep it covered just as we do. How could an animal get inside unless it was deliberately thrown in?"

"We have no idea how it happened," said Raka. All of the wrinkles in his face were rigid. "It's possible that someone might have been careless and is now too scared to admit it."

"Have you anything to add to this, Tara?" said Kripan, staring at her with open dislike.

Tara was glad he was not Morni's chief. He was so rude *and* he had barged into their village in the middle of the night, demanding a resolution. Already the tension between him and Raka was mounting. But was Raka strong enough to protect her and Morni? Of late he seemed so easily swayed by people's opinions instead of following his own heart.

"We're waiting, Tara," said Kripan. "We don't have all the time in the world."

Mirthless laughter bubbled up inside Tara at his words. She almost laughed aloud at the truth in his words, but caught herself in time. "At the time our well was contaminated, I was in the temple day and night, scrubbing every inch of it in preparation for the pooja. You can ask Punditji if you like."

All eyes turned to Punditji, who sat in the front row with an umbrella. The sun climbed higher, scorching the ground and cooking the people who squatted on it.

"Punditji?" said Raka.

The priest wiped his flabby face with a white cloth that hung over his shoulder, but did not say a word.

"We need an answer, Punditji. Could Tara have contaminated the well?"

"She could have sneaked away while I was asleep ..."

"That's not true!" said Tara. She glared at Punditji. "Each time you came back from your numerous naps, I was cleaning a different section of the temple. You even mentioned that it was going faster than expected. If I had sneaked away, you would have known."

Punditji's face resembled an overripe tomato.

"Yes ... hmmm, she probably did stay in the temple all the time," he replied. "She couldn't have done it."

"So then let's talk about *our* well," said Kripan.

Tara looked at Raka. "I didn't do it. I was nowhere close to the well."

"Then where were you all of yesterday?" asked Raka.

A loud silence filled the clearing. Tara stared at him, remembering the events of the last few hours; the cold desolation of the Underworld, the whispers of the dead, the cuts on her palms, and the words of Zarku and Kali. All of that had been futile. She had still lost her brother.

"Our house had just burned down," said Tara. Her eyes flicked to Layla, who stared back unblinkingly. "We lost everything and Suraj ..." Her voice faltered as his small body, covered in her sunshine-yellow dupatta strayed into her mind. "Suraj was badly burned and NOW HE'S DEAD!"

A fly buzzed overhead. No other sound broke the silence. Tara hadn't meant to say that, not here, not in front of everyone. It had just burst out of her.

Raka shot to his feet. "Are you sure, Tara?"

"Would I lie about my brother's death?" she replied, deeply regretting having mentioned it now. Almost every face was devoid of sadness or emotion.

"Where is he?" asked Raka.

"With mother, where ... where you last saw us," said Tara. It had been at the tip of her tongue to say it was where he had locked them up. But she needed his support right now. It would be foolish to anger her only ally.

Raka sat down with a deep sigh. "I'm so very sorry to hear this, Tara. We will take care of things as soon as this is over."

Other members of Morni's Panchayat murmured their apologies.

"That still does not answer my question," said Kripan. "Where were you all of yesterday?"

"I told you," said Tara. "I was upset and worried. We had lost everything. I went for a walk, *alone*, to think things over. I was far away from Pinjaur. I must have lost track of the time because when I returned, I heard Suraj was in a bad state. I ran to get the vaid and when he refused to come, I went to Rakaji to ask for help."

"Then how do you explain your cooking pot, which was found near the well, and that someone saw you run away," said Kripan.

"Someone saw a *child* run away," said Tara. "Call Layla. We'll find out the truth in a minute."

"What is she talking about?" said Kripan. "Who's Layla?"

Raka looked at Tara for a moment. Then he spoke. "Layla, come up here, please."

Layla jumped to her feet and bounded to the front, as if she'd been summoned for a performance. And Tara was sure it would be a performance to remember, complete with tears, dramatics, and anything else she could think of, to gain the sympathy of the villagers.

The only good thing was that Layla was now within reach. Tara stared at her fat neck as Layla strutted up and stood beside her. All she needed was a few minutes without any intervention and it would be over. Tara squinted up at the blinding sun. She still had a few hours to carry out her plan.

"Layla, don't you have a kurta in the same green material as I do? Mother had it stitched for both of us at the same time," said Tara. She knew the answer, but she asked the question anyway.

"No," said Layla.

"You're lying!" said Tara. "Where have you hidden yours?"

"I knew you would take that line," said Layla. Her

lips quivered and her hands trembled as she spread them, beseeching the crowd. "Why would I lie about this? Parvati and Shiv took me in, but they treated me like an *orphan*. They fed me crumbs, made me work in the house all day, and gave me Tara's old clothes to wear …" Layla paused to wipe an imaginary tear, sniffing hard.

Tara snorted. "Two of me would fit into the clothes *you* wear, and as for crumbs, they must have been very large if you could grow to this size."

"Enough of this drama," said Kripan. "What's the point of calling her here, Tara?"

"She's the one who should be punished, not me. Our house burned down. Everything that wasn't destroyed was lying in the open. Anyone could have picked up a pot and dropped it near the well. Layla has a green shalwar-kurta, but she's probably destroyed it by now. Has anyone asked Layla where *she* was yesterday? And did the villager who claims he saw a child near the well get a look at the child's face?"

Tara glanced over at Layla and thought she looked a bit pale. A tiny bubble of hope blossomed inside her. She might still be able to clear her name before she left Morni forever.

"I saw her," said someone from the crowd. All eyes turned toward the speaker.

An old, stick-thin man rose from the crowd. His face was badly scarred and disfigured with burn marks, reminding Tara of Suraj. She shuddered and looked away.

"You saw her face?" asked Kripan. "Are you absolutely sure?"

The old man hobbled to the front with a pronounced limp. His thumb and forefinger rubbed against each other; an involuntary gesture that he was quite unaware of. His long, greasy hair framed his gaunt face. Tara stared at him. Why did he seem so familiar?

The old man returned her stare as he passed. She had seen this man somewhere before, but she just couldn't remember where.

"What is your name?" asked Raka.

The old man bowed and folded his hands. "Dayalu."

"What do you do for a living?"

"Odd jobs. I grow vegetables in my garden and sell or trade them for food."

"What happened to your face?" asked Raka.

"Ahhh, that's a long story. It was a terrible fire."

"Continue," said Raka.

"I am willing to swear before God, and may I be afflicted with the worst disease possible if I have lied, Tara is the person I saw. This is what happened —"

"NO!" said Tara. "He's lying."

"Shut up," snarled Kripan. "One more word out of you and we'll pronounce you guilty without listening to anyone else."

Tara looked toward Raka, but his face was blank. The bubble within her burst. If Raka believed she was guilty, then there was no hope for her.

She scanned the crowd for a friendly face, but there was none. Gayatri would definitely not be here, not unless she wanted to be insulted by the Panchayat yet again. And Suraj would never go anywhere, ever again. Tara thought of him lying in Raka's kitchen, with only one person to mourn his brief life and almost broke down. She tried to focus on her elder brother who was still alive.

But why wasn't Ananth here? She scanned the crowd, again and again, but no, he was missing. Had she lost two brothers instead of one? Had he turned against her, too?

The old man was going into infinite detail about his day's activities and the crowd shifted restlessly. With great effort, Tara focused on listening to him wondering who would vouch for her because it seemed like there was no one left in the village who would stand by her side.

"Hurry up, Dayalu," said Raka, reading her mind. "Get straight to the part when you saw Tara."

"All right," said the old man in a huff. "It was afternoon and my water had run out. I had barely a cupful left. It was so hot that I hated to get out of the house. But it was that or die of thirst. How was I to know that I would be thirsty for a long, long time?" He licked his cracked lips and paused. His thumb and forefinger rubbed against each other.

"Then?" prompted Kripan.

"I stepped out of my hut. The earth burned my feet. The streets were deserted. No one was stupid enough to venture out in the heat. Even the villagers who guard the well were taking a break. I walked toward the well." He stopped again. Everyone leaned forward.

How elaborately he was spinning these lies and the crowd was hanging on to his every word! For the umpteenth time, Tara wished she hadn't promised Lord Yama that she wouldn't tell anyone about their journey. How simple it would be if she could tell them the truth and see the shock and shame on their faces when they realized she was a hero and not someone to be hated.

"That's when I saw her," Dayalu said. "She was leaning over the edge, looking in. I was happy there was someone to help. I can't lift heavy things these days. I walked as fast as my old legs would allow me."

Layla listened intently to every word the old man uttered and so did all the villagers. *How had she put a stranger up to it*, thought Tara, *and why would he lie for her?* There had to be a connection somewhere and she had to find it before it was too late. She observed the two of them closely, especially Layla. The looks between them were neutral, but Tara was sure they knew each other. Now and then Layla would nod, almost imperceptibly, as the old man spoke. It dawned on Tara; they were enacting a well-rehearsed play. If the Panchayat chose to believe the old man, she would be dead before Yama came for her. The thought made her go icy cold.

Would that be such a bad thing? the small voice within her asked. *At least you won't spend the rest of your life in the Underworld.* But that also meant Layla would go free. No, that couldn't happen. Layla had killed Suraj and she would have to pay, even if it meant Tara would have to spend the rest of her life in limbo. But she would have to move fast.

"I drew nearer. I saw her lean over. There was a loud splash," Dayalu continued. "Stop, I called out to her. What are you doing?' The moment she saw me, she dropped the pot she was carrying, covered her face with her dupatta and ran away."

"That's a lie!" said Tara.

Kripan and Raka both glared at her.

"When I reached the well, she was gone," said the old man. He swept his sleeve over his damp forehead. "I looked inside and couldn't see anything. My eyesight is not what it used to be. I pulled up a bucket of water. Nothing came up, but I knew she had thrown something that shouldn't be in there. Surely no one would throw rocks into the well in the middle of the afternoon for the fun of it."

He paused again, his hand on his chest, but Tara knew it was an act. He was enjoying every moment of this, drawing it out as much as he could.

The rocks are all in your head, thought Tara, but this time she dared not speak aloud. The sun scorched the back of her neck and sweat trickled down between her shoulder blades. She was starting to feel light-headed.

"I knew something was wrong," said Dayalu. "I threw the water back into the well and drew out another bucketful. My back was aching and my arms were ready to fall off, but I could not rest. The second bucket brought up nothing. It was the third bucket that brought it up …" He stopped mid-sentence and surveyed the crowd. No one shifted. No one spoke.

"What was it?" asked Raka. "Stop being so dramatic and speak quickly or sit down."

The old man sneered at Raka. "The third bucket brought up the carcass of a diseased dog. It was badly slashed and still bleeding. It's a good thing that I did not take a sip of water or I wouldn't be here today."

For a long minute, no one spoke. They all stared at the old man and then at her. No one even glanced at Layla.

Raka cleared his throat. "You're absolutely certain you saw Tara's face before she ran away? This is a matter of a child's life and you cannot make a mistake."

The old man's eyes bored into Tara's, his thumb and forefinger rubbing against each other again. "Yes," he said.

The crowd gasped as one.

"You may go now," said Raka.

The old man hobbled back to his place. Tara watched his receding back, the feeling stronger than ever that she knew this old man. But her brain was so full of all the things she had to worry about, she just couldn't put her finger on it.

"We have a culprit and now we have the witness,"

said Kripan, unable to conceal the joy in his voice. "Now all that remains is the sentencing."

"Not so fast, Kripan," said Raka. "I'd like to give Tara one more chance to speak."

Kripan swore under his breath and glanced at the other members of his Panchayat. One of them nodded. "Very well," said Kripan. "But she had better keep it short."

"Tara, what do you have to say about Dayalu's testimony?" said Raka.

"It's a complete lie," said Tara. The acrid smell of her sweat was making her sick.

"And Dayalu didn't see you?"

"No," said Tara.

"Why won't you tell us where you really were? What are you hiding from us?"

Every nerve within Tara twisted into knots. This was her very last chance. Should she break her promise to Lord Yama and clear her name, or remain silent and face a death sentence? What was the punishment for breaking a promise to God?

Help me Lord Ganesh, thought Tara, surveying the accusing faces that surrounded her. But there was no reply, no sign at all. The decision was hers and hers alone.

Raka seemed to sense her dilemma. His expression softened a little. "Don't be afraid, Tara. Your life depends on what you say next. Can you just tell us the truth?"

Tara took a deep breath and opened her mouth.

twenty-four

Framed and a Failure

"No," said Tara. "I can't."

"She should be sentenced right away!" said Kripan. "How can you tolerate such insolence from a child, Raka? No wonder Morni is in trouble."

Raka flushed. "I'll thank you not to talk to me about *my* village, Kripan. Yours is in no better shape. Let's not forget the trouble you had because of the zemindars raising the taxes."

It was Kripan's turn to flush. He pretended to consult one of his Panchayat members in a low voice.

"We need to discuss this one more time," said Raka. "A child's life is at stake and besides, Tara is Prabala's granddaughter. We cannot sentence her until we are absolutely sure or we'll have to face his wrath when he gets back."

"Where is Prabala?" asked a member of Pinjaur's

Panchayat. "Shouldn't he be here?"

"He's in the Himalayas, meditating," said Raka in an apologetic voice. "Tara's father, Shiv, has gone to bring him back. He was the one who had saved us from the Vetalas. He and Tara, both. That is why I just cannot understand this behaviour. It's so unlike her." He massaged his temples, his expression troubled.

"People change, especially when they're possessed," said Kripan. "If you're too weak, I can see this through, Raka."

"I'm *not* possessed, Layla is!" shouted Tara. "Why am I the only one who can see this?"

"There you go again, trying to find someone else to blame," said Kripan. "We have a witness, Tara, so you can't lie anymore. If you were in my village, by now —"

"But she's not," snapped Raka. "She's a part of Morni and we take care of our own problems. Let's discuss this in private." He stood up. "The rest of you, go back to what you were doing. The meeting is adjourned until tonight. If we reach a decision sooner, we'll send a message to everyone."

"Yes," said Kripan. "Everyone from Pinjaur, go back and get some work done."

There was grumbling and muttering as the crowd got to its feet and started shuffling away. Raka was talking to Kartik, and Kripan consulted with his team.

They seemed to have forgotten that Tara was still standing there waiting for instructions. And so was Layla.

Tara took a step toward Layla, one thought burning in the darkness that filled her soul: *kill her*. She even had Zarku's dagger to finish the job properly.

Layla must have sensed her thoughts. She took a step back, eyeing Tara warily.

The men were still busy talking. Tara grabbed Layla's arm. "Come with me, quietly," she said, her heart doing the Tandav in her chest. If only she could walk Layla a short distance away from anyone who might intervene, she would be able complete what she'd set out to do. After that she would accept her fate happily. "I have to talk to you about … about your mother. It's urgent."

Layla ripped her arm out of Tara's grasp. "Leave me alone. HELP!" she yelled.

Immediately a couple of villagers pulled her away and Tara bit her lip to stop from crying. Her chances of carrying out the plan were fading fast.

"Take her to an empty hut and lock her up," said Raka. "Make sure she gets some food."

Tara dug her heels into the ground as they started to drag her away. "Please, Rakaji, can I see my mother? I-I need to talk to her." She almost added, "for the last time."

Raka shook his head. "Tara, you're on trial here. I don't know if it has sunk in yet, but you're in a lot of trouble. Because of you, thousands of lives are in jeopardy, and the punishment for that is death by stoning."

Tara stared at him mutely. Her skin crawled as she imagined stones flying at her from all directions, the pain in her body and soul as she died in the street like a rabid dog, watched and reviled by all.

"Five minutes is all I need," said Tara, hating the pleading note that had crept into her voice.

"No," said Raka. "You will remain in the hut until we have made our decision. You will have a chance to say your goodbyes after the sentencing."

Tara lunged forward and grasped his arm. "You don't understand, Rakaji. I also have one last job to complete. I must speak with Layla alone and after that I promise, I will do whatever you ask of me. Please, trust in me one last time."

Raka shook her arm off and walked away. Tara stared after him, curses teetering on her lips. Her heart was a stone in her chest. He was not the strong, fair man he used to be. Time and circumstance had weakened him.

Tara turned to run, but the villagers grabbed her once more.

"Let me go," she screamed. Their grip tightened.

Around her, everyone watched the spectacle; some with pity and some with disgust. Layla stood a short distance away, well out of reach. There was a look of such triumph on her face that Tara's insides churned with misery and all the fight seeped out of her.

As they made their way through Morni, more villagers stopped to ogle at her. Tara looked neither left nor right, and concentrated on putting one foot in front of the other.

When they reached the hut, the men pushed her inside a little harder than was necessary. She stumbled into the empty room and turned around. The door slammed in her face.

Tara ran into the second room. It was bare and the back door was boarded up. The only way in and out was through the front door. She stared at the lone window in the room, high up on the wall. No one could have escaped through that. Not even Kabir. Thinking of him and her friends made her lonelier than ever.

Tara slid to the ground, hugged her knees to her chest, and closed her eyes. The day flashed through her mind. She had lost Suraj forever, she had stood trial for crimes she had not committed, and had earned the hatred of every single villager at the meeting today. And now she was locked up, unable to carry out the one task she had come back to finish.

A ray of sunlight slid across the floor and touched the tips of her mojris. Tara watched the golden finger through blurry eyes. Everyone had taken leave of their senses, but what about Ananth? He must believe she was guilty, too, because he had not shown his face at all. The thought was like a punch to the stomach. She didn't care if all of Morni and Pinjaur found her guilty, but not her own brother! How could he have given up on her without even hearing her side of the story?

The tears came then, soaking her shalwar. She lay down, her cheek pressed to the mud floor.

The front door opened and there was a metallic clang. "Eat!" someone said. Almost immediately the door banged shut.

She couldn't even think of eating, but she got up anyway, and peeked into the front room. A thali containing a single paratha, and crowned with flies, sat by the door. There was no water. She was not surprised. They were already punishing her by keeping her thirsty.

Tara sat down again, thankful for the solitary ray of sunshine that kept her company when everyone else had abandoned her. Something else was nagging her: the old man. Why had he lied for Layla? Had Kripan and his Panchayat colluded against her? But why? She had never harmed them. It made no sense....

Tara closed her eyes and drew in a deep, long breath of humid air. She thought of Dayalu again, with his greasy hair, and the curious movement of his thumb and forefinger rubbing against each other, as if he were counting money. She jerked upright, her eyes snapping open. Of course! There was one other person who used to do this; Dushta, the moneylender, Kali's father. They all believed he had perished in the battle between the Vetalas and Lord Yama, but he had somehow escaped! Because of his disfigurement and the amount of weight he had lost, no one had recognized him. But when Tara recalled his face, she was sure it was him. Of course he would lie for his daughter and granddaughter. It made perfect sense now. *And it was proof that she was innocent.*

Tara jumped to her feet, raced to the front door and pounded on it, ignoring her palms, which throbbed painfully. "Open up!" she yelled. "I have very important information for Raka."

No one answered her. Where were they all? Tara ran to a small window beside the front door, pressed her forehead to the bars and peered out. There was no one around. They had locked her up and gone away.

"I have some important information!" yelled Tara. "Someone call Raka. Get a message to him, please...."

No one answered her plea and even if they heard her yell, they chose to ignore it.

Tara screamed until she was hoarse, but not a soul appeared. It was like being in the Underworld again where the louder she screamed, the less her chances of being heard. She shuffled back into the room and lay down, tired beyond belief. She looked at the scabs on her palms; stark reminders of what she had done for Morni. No one would ever know.

Grief and anger pummelled her insides so that she was unable to rest or sleep. She lay on the floor, watching the ray of sunshine move higher and higher up the wall as the sun sank into the horizon.

She had failed. Miserably.

twenty-five

The Final Verdict

"**I**t's time to go." The voice came from far away. "Up, now!"

Someone prodded her roughly and Tara sat up, her heart beating wildly. "Wha-what happened?"

"The Panchayats have reached a decision," said the villager.

Tara got to her feet and glanced outside. Night was upon them. She had slept the day away. Lord Yama would be coming for her in a few hours. Everything that had happened in the last twenty-four hours came flooding back, along with the crushing disappointment that it was too late to carry out her plan. Layla would live and she would die.

"Come on, move," said the villager. "We can't keep them waiting."

Tara ran her hands through her messy hair, trying to

control their shaking. "Let's go."

• • •

Lanterns were placed at regular intervals on the raised platform in the centre of the village. Flickering torches circled the periphery of the clearing. Smoke from the torches rose into the air and hung in a black cloud over them.

Morni's Panchayat was already seated on the platform. Kripan was there, too, but a couple of members of his Panchayat were still missing. Most of the villagers had gathered and more poured in. It seemed that no one wanted to miss her sentencing.

Row upon row of curious onlookers craned their necks as she walked to the front of the crowd and faced them. Some jeered and spit at her while others followed her with accusing eyes.

Tara was once again reminded of Kali's trial. The crowd had been half the size then. Little had she known that the decision made on that day would come to haunt her years later. If only her mother could have predicted this, they would have banished Layla, too. Instead, they had raised a poisonous snake in their midst who had turned on them at the first opportunity.

Once again, she scanned the crowd for the one face she longed to see, the one person who could not fail her. And this time she saw Ananth at the back of the crowd.

Her heart leaped. He had come out to support her!

As Tara stared at him, an idea took shape in her mind. Why shouldn't she ask *him* to finish the task? Kill Layla to rid them of Kali's evil legacy once and for all. The huge boulder that sat on her chest became lighter. There was still a chance that this could work out.

She stared at Ananth and jerked her head slightly, hoping he'd understand her and come closer. He stared back at her with a blank face. A boy in the front row spat on her. Tara glared at him. When she looked up again, Ananth was gone. She searched the crowd, unable to believe what she was seeing. But it was true. Ananth had vanished.

It was as if someone had put a lit match to her heart. Ananth had abandoned her, too.

Tara faced the Panchayat. All ten now sat on the platform, staring at her with grim expressions. Her gaze travelled along the front row and there was Layla smirking at her. Tara looked away, too miserable to even muster a glare.

"Is everyone here?" asked Raka.

Someone replied that more villagers from Pinjaur were expected.

Tara scanned the crowd for Dayalu and was not surprised to find him missing. He had helped his granddaughter; his job was done. Why hadn't she recognized him earlier? Things might have turned out differently for her. Would anyone believe her if she told them now?

"I have something to say," said Tara, addressing Raka. "It's very important."

"You had your chance earlier, Tara. I don't want to hear a single word from you. Now you will listen to what *we* have to say."

Tara looked away, her face burning. She blinked back tears, refusing to let him or anyone else have the satisfaction of seeing her cry. Someone coughed loudly, drawing her attention. It was Layla. She mouthed the word *suffer* and smiled. Tara longed to stick the dagger, which was still in her pocket, into Layla's heart and twist it.

But the thought of attempting it in front of so many people made her sick. And she knew she'd never succeed.

The crowd swelled and the clearing was at bursting capacity. How could so many people hate her?

Raka stood up and raised his hand. Immediately the villagers became silent. A few children raced up and sat in front of Layla, who was now safely ensconced within the crowd. It would be impossible to get to her and Tara forced herself to drop the idea and focus on Raka. Her heart was working extra hard and she was afraid it would stop beating any moment.

"Thank you all for your patience. We have finally reached a decision."

Tara clasped her sweaty hands together. Up until this moment her one desire had been to kill Layla. She had not given a second's thought to her own fate. And now she was about to find out how she would die unless Lord Yama claimed her first. Either way she was doomed; to a painful death or eternal misery in the Underworld.

"Kripan will make the announcement," said Raka.

Kripan stood up. His eyes travelled the crowd slowly, so slowly that it seemed he was looking at each and every person. Tara wrung her hands. The tight knots in her neck and shoulders ached. She wished he would hurry up.

"We have decided that Tara's crimes have seriously affected us all; our families, our crops, our very existence," said Kripan. "That is a grave sin."

"So what's the verdict?" someone called out from the crowd.

Kripan looked straight at her. "Tara will be stoned to death."

"NOOOOO!" someone screeched from the back of the crowd. "You can't do that to my child!"

Tara's head whipped round though she knew exactly who had yelled out. "Mother!"

Parvati pushed through the crowd and stumbled into Tara's arms.

"Oh my poor child," she said, hugging Tara tight.

A spiraling panic seeped through Tara and there was nothing she could do to stop it. She held on to her mother, wishing she had the power to make time stand still. She didn't want to die ... not by stoning. And definitely not now!

"Parvati, you should not be here," said Raka. He got off the parapet and came toward them.

"Stay away from my daughter, you senile old man," screamed Parvati. "You have no idea how wrong you are about this brave child of mine. She wouldn't harm a fly."

Raka's face turned grimmer. He nodded to two villagers close by. "Take her back to my hut and make sure she stays there."

The men advanced on Tara and her mother. Tara tightened her grip. They caught hold of Parvati's arms and pulled her away, but it felt as if they had torn Tara's heart out. Parvati was sobbing like a child. Tara knew that if she cried or showed her despair, it would drive her mother mad.

She swallowed the bitter taste of fear and tried to control the panic that now raced through her veins, becoming part of every breath she took.

Tara walked up to her and cupped her face. "Mother, I'll be all right. Go back to Suraj. Please."

Parvati's face was contorted with pain as she stared at Tara. She opened her mouth but no words came out.

"They're making a huge mistake but they will realize it very soon," said Tara. "We Lalls are strong and I'm not going to beg or plead for mercy."

"Then I will," said Parvati. "I'll do anything to save your life."

"No, Mother. I don't want you to let go of your

dignity in front of these people. You must go. Lord Ganesh is with me."

The two villagers Raka had summoned stood close by, looking ashamed. Neither could meet her eye. They tugged at Parvati once more. She broke free and lunged at Tara, embracing her fiercely. This time Tara did not return the hug though she inhaled deeply, capturing the scent of her mother within her heart. Then she took another deep breath. She was not going to give this blind, superstitious crowd the satisfaction of seeing her break down.

"Please go, Mother," said Tara quietly. "And don't come back, no matter what you hear."

Parvati fainted and Tara had to use every bit of willpower to keep from rushing to her side. The villagers carried her away, leaving Tara with the memory of her stricken face.

"When are you ... when will this happen?" said Tara trying to control the tremble in her voice.

"Now," said Raka. He could barely meet her eye. Tara glanced at the villagers who had once been like family, but no longer.

Think of the upside, the little voice piped in. *You'll be like all the other dead in the Underworld instead of wandering around, alive and lonely.* And yet, this was not the way she wanted to go. Her pride smarted as she realized that she was the first child in the history of Morni to die this way. Forever after, her family name, the name of the Lalls, would be despised.

The crowd was moving back. Some of the villagers from Pinjaur were tossing something into the air, catching it again deftly. Rocks! They were already armed.

Tara clenched her hands. A voice she hated intensely whispered into her ear.

"Told you I'd win."

twenty-six

Death by Stoning

A low hum started within the crowd and spread rapidly like a forest fire.

Tara tensed, her stomach heaving, her head spinning. Who would throw the first stone? How much would it hurt? The villagers, armed with rocks, now pressed closer. The members of the Panchayats were also standing. Tara had never experienced a stoning before, but that was about to change.

For a moment there was hushed silence. Were they waiting for a command from the Panchayat? Were they waiting for her to cry, to run? Then the rumbling began.

'Kill her," someone said.

"Stone the witch," another yelled.

"She must die!" A woman shrieked.

Tara's knees turned to jelly as the voices grew more strident. Her lungs seemed empty even though she took deep breaths. The edges of her vision start to blur.

The next moment Tara's head exploded with pain. She screamed and clapped her hand to her head. It came away moist and red. Someone had thrown the first stone.

She scanned the crowd, blood streaming down her face, and wasn't surprised when Layla stepped forward.

"What are you all waiting for?" screamed Layla. "This evil person deserves to die!"

The floodgates opened and rocks flew at her from all sides, connecting with bone and tender skin. Tara shrieked and fell to the ground covering her head. Tears of anger, pain, and shame coursed down her cheeks as a monsoon of rocks rained down. She was on fire and prayed one of the rocks would knock her unconscious.

"STOP!" roared a voice filled with rage.

The voice boomed through the village centre. Immediately the shower of stones stopped. Tara tried to stand, but it was too painful. She managed to sit up, all of her screaming in agony. Blood trickled into her right eye so that she could barely see clearly.

The clip-clopping of hooves and loud gasps that rippled through the crowd gave away her rescuer's identity. Villagers jumped aside and Lord Yama rode straight up to her. He dismounted and helped Tara to her feet. "You're late, Tara and now I know why. I'm so sorry I didn't get here sooner. Oh my dear child, just look at you …"

Tara shook her head, unable to say a word. His kindness was too much to bear and the tears continued to flow. He shook his large head sorrowfully and wiped her tears.

"I failed, Lord Yama. I failed."

Yama glanced at Layla, who stood in the front row staring at them, aghast. He turned to the Panchayats. "Have you all taken complete leave of your senses? You're killing the one person who is trying to save you? You're all weak, foolish, and PATHETIC!"

The crowd drew back. Only Raka stood his ground.

"Lord Yama," he said, folding his hands, "we did not expect to see you here. But with all due respect, you are wrong. Tara has committed terrible crimes that have ruined the livelihood of many. The effects of her actions will be felt not just by Morni, but Pinjaur, too, for months to come. She has upset the gods with her wickedness and we're all paying for it. The monsoon has failed and our crops are dead. Yesterday, she was up to her cruel tricks in Pinjaur and this time we have a witness."

"She wasn't even in your world yesterday, let alone Pinjaur," said Lord Yama. "Tara was in the Underworld, trying to talk sense into Kali to save your miserable hides. I know it because I took her there and brought her back."

The collective gasp of the crowd was music to Tara's ears. At last, they knew the truth. The truth that she had struggled to keep to herself because of her promise to Lord Yama. She scanned the crowd, but no one met her eyes.

Raka mopped his streaming white face with his turban. "But then who did that old man, Dayalu, see at the well? He swore he saw Tara. Are you saying he was lying?"

Lord Yama reached out a massive hand and plucked Layla from the front row. "*This* is the bad egg. She's been acting on the instructions of her mother, Kali, and wreaking havoc with all your lives."

"That can't be true," said Raka. His voice shook and broke. "It's not possible ..."

"In all the time that you have known Tara, have you ever seen her kill anything or hurt anyone?" said Yama.

Raka shook his head.

"Then how could you believe she could contaminate not one, but two wells harming hundreds of people?"

"But the evidence —" Raka started to say.

"Can be tampered with," snapped Lord Yama. "Who vanquished Zarku and saved you all from a fate worse than death?"

"Tara," said Raka in a very small voice.

"Who brought Suraj and Sadia back at great peril to her own life?"

This time Raka could not reply. He swallowed hard.

"Tara!" said Yama. "How could you even *think* she could be guilty? Just because you found an article of clothing and a pot at the sites of the crimes? Raka, I thought the Panchayat was wise and you more so, but you've disappointed me today. You have made such a huge mistake."

Raka flushed. "We thought that because she'd spent so much time with Zarku, his evil influence —"

"Are you mad?" said Yama. "You let superstition guide your actions? I'm appalled at your stupidity."

"But then why didn't she tell us the truth?" said Raka. "Why did she stay silent? We gave her the chance to speak yesterday. She said she went for a walk all alone. We all knew that was a lie!"

Lord Yama came up to Tara and wiped her cheeks gently. He looked at the blood smeared on his hand and shook his head once again. "Why didn't you tell them, Tara?"

"I gave you my word that I wouldn't," said Tara softly.

Lord Yama patted her head. "You are a star, Tara. In all my time, I have never seen someone as brave and true as you."

Yama turned around to face the Raka. "I had made Tara promise not to tell anyone where she had been. It would have ruined the balance in the world and would have angered some gods. All she was doing was keeping her word, even though it meant she would have to pay for the silence with her life. You should touch her feet, Raka, and worship her instead of stoning her to death. That goes for all of you."

Raka's eyes darted to Kripan, who looked defiant and then back to Lord Yama. Finally he looked at Tara. "On behalf of the Panchayat, please accept our apology. We have made a huge mistake."

"YES, YOU HAVE!" said Yama. "All of you missed the real culprit, Layla, even though Tara tried to warn you several times."

Tara turned to see Layla's reaction, but she wasn't there. While he and Raka were talking she had slipped into the crowd.

Tara ignored the agonizing pain that made it hard to move even a muscle and dove into the crowd. She caught Layla by her pigtail and dragged her back to the front. Layla squealed, trying to break free. Not a single villager helped her. Tara hung on to her with every bit of strength she had. With Yama next to her, she could finally complete what she had set out to do. And this time no one would dare stop her.

"Please," said Layla. "I'm just a child. You can't hurt me."

"But you were willing to hurt another child?" said Yama, towering over her. "In all my years I have not come across anyone like you, Layla. You have put the most corrupt souls to shame because you have done so much harm to so many, at such a young age. I dread to think what you'll be capable of when you grow up."

Tara addressed the Panchayat. "This is exactly what I've been telling everyone. Kali's last words to me were that Layla would avenge her death and she was right. That's why I requested Lord Yama to take me to the Underworld to meet Kali, to stop her from influencing her daughter. But it was futile. Kali said she'd stop only after I was dead and she'd taken revenge on each and every villager in Morni who had wronged her."

"So then ... all of those terrible things that happened in Morni; the wells, the butchered dog in the temple," asked Raka. "That was *you*, Layla?"

Layla looked from Raka to Lord Yama and finally to Tara. She chewed her nails but did not utter a word.

"You'd better speak up," said Tara. She wanted Layla to confess in front of all the villagers so that her name would be clear.

Layla shook her head.

Tara wrapped her hands around Layla's fat neck; an act she had dreamed of for so long. Terror sprang into Layla's eyes and Tara's grip slackened involuntarily as she realized what she was really doing. She was cold-bloodedly murdering a child!

Layla seemed to sense her thoughts. The terror in her eyes receded. Layla was expecting her to show mercy as always. But then, Suraj's face popped into her head. Tara remembered his small hand in hers, growing cold while she had argued with her mother. Because of Layla she would never hear him call her *Didi* again. Her hands tightened and she stepped closer, their faces inches apart. No one attempted to intervene.

"I want the Panchayat to hear this, Layla. Who put the dead dog in the temple and framed me?" said Tara.

"I-I don't ..." Layla stuttered. Tara squeezed hard and the answer popped out of Layla.

"I did it," said Layla. "Let me go now."

The villagers muttered audibly.

"Why did you do something so terrible, Layla?" said Raka. He stepped closer and stared at Layla as if she were a particularly loathsome insect. "Even if you hated Tara, why would our defile the temple? Have you no respect for God, for the rest of us?"

Layla struggled to break free. Tara slapped her hard. Layla stopped twitching, her eyes glittering with rage.

"I'm not finished yet, Rakaji," said Tara. "Who contaminated Morni's well water?"

Layla stared at Tara. Sweat beaded her forehead and her lower lip quivered. The livid crowd hurled curses at her.

"Evil spawn of an evil mother!"

"You miserable wretch."

"Give her the same punishment we gave Tara: stone her to death!"

"I asked you a question," said Tara in a cold voice. Her arms were starting to ache and she didn't know how much longer she'd be able to hold on.

"You know the answer so stop asking silly questions," said Layla. "Mother and I still communicate. She came up with the plans and I carried them out. We never expected to be caught."

Tara's relief was so great that she almost let go of Layla. She had finally cleared her name; the granddaughter of Prabala had not ruined the family name of the Lalls.

An ashen-faced Sumathy emerged from the crowd. She came up to them and slapped Layla hard. "You are your mother's daughter all right," said Sumathy. "We looked after you and all along you were the cause of all our troubles. You've ruined my belief in the innocence of childhood."

Layla spit in her face and Sumathy was so shocked that she stood still, saliva dripping down her cheeks.

"Who was that old man who said he saw me by the well at Pinjaur?" said Tara, eager to remove any doubt from the villagers' minds.

"I know you've figured it out," said Layla. "So why don't you show the villagers how clever you are. If you want to throw me out of the village, go ahead and do it. I don't care!"

Tara shook her so hard that her head snapped back and forth.

"Stop … you're hurting me," said Layla.

Lord Yama stepped up closer. "You better answer that, Layla." He said it very quietly but his tone was stern and forbidding.

"It was Dushta, my grandfather," said Layla. A sullen expression replaced the ever-present smirk on her pasty face.

This time the crowd didn't even gasp. They were just as shocked as she had been when she'd realized that Kali's father was still alive, and that he had aided his granddaughter in giving false testimony.

Raka beckoned to a couple of villagers. "Mangu, Hari, go and find him, now," he said. "Bring him back. He will be severely punished for his part in this scheme." The villagers loped off immediately.

"I have one last question, Layla," said Tara. "I know the answer, but I still want to hear it from you. Why did you set fire to my hut? You hated *me*, not my family, so why did you take Suraj away from me?"

Layla stared at her for a moment and then laughed. "I would love to take credit for it, but it wasn't me."

Tara dug her fingers into Layla's windpipe. Layla gasped and choked but she still managed to croak. "Not me."

"Don't you dare lie to me," said Tara. Anger gave her strength and she squeezed harder. "Admit it. You killed my brother!"

Layla's eyes bulged with terror and she gasped. "Not. Me."

"Let her go," said a voice that was as familiar to her as her heartbeat.

"I did it," he said.

twenty-seven

Revelations and Regrets

Tara's hands dropped to her sides. She turned around very slowly and faced Ananth.

His face was a mask of stone. "I am the culprit."

"Why?" whispered Tara. "*Why?*" She was shivering so violently that it was difficult to speak. She sank to the ground, not taking her eyes off Ananth, wishing Lord Yama had taken her away before she had asked this question. "Did Layla force you to do this?"

Ananth looked away once again and now Tara understood why he hadn't been able to meet her eyes. It was *his* guilt, not hers, which made him avoid her.

Layla shrieked with laughter. "I wish I could say this was my plan, but it wasn't. Your brother did this by himself. Bravo, Ananth!"

"Not by himself," said another voice Tara knew well. "He was following instructions."

She closed her eyes and held her aching head in her hands. So this was the surprise Kali and Zarku had been laughing about. But it could not be real. She was having a nightmare and when she awoke, she would be in her bed and everything would be all right.

"I told him to do this," said Raka in a shaky voice. "It was the Panchayat's decision and we were wrong."

The last vestiges of respect for Morni, and its Panchayat, evaporated. Tara had known Raka all her life and yet, she realized, she did not know him at all. He had been the pillar of strength for the people of Morni. *For her.* Only now she saw how many cracks had appeared in that pillar. It was crumbling.

"You *asked* Ananth to set fire to our home?" said Tara. "Why?"

Raka took a deep breath. "The Panchayat was under a lot of pressure from the villagers," he said. "They believed that if you and your family were gone from Morni it would rid us of all the bad luck we were having. You've been too close to Zarku and we all believed that you brought his evil home to us. With you gone, the drought would be over. Peace and prosperity would return to Morni."

Tara gulped. Her throat was so tight, she could barely speak. "You listened to them? I saved you all from Zarku and you thought *I* was bad luck for the village?"

Raka did not say a word, but the answer was on his face.

"And you decided to get rid of us while my father and grandfather were away? You chose to attack us in the middle of the night, Raka?" She couldn't address him with the respectful "ji" ever again.

"As I said, I was under a lot of pressure," said Raka. "The villagers …"

Tara got to her feet and gazed at the villagers who looked anywhere but at her.

"Why did you choose my brother for the job, Raka?" said Tara. "And how could you agree, Ananth?"

"Because the Panchayat threatened to go through the Sati ceremony for my mother if I didn't do as I was told," said Ananth. "They said she was adding to the bad fortune of the villagers. I couldn't bear to lose her. I'm so very sorry, Tara. No one was happier than I that you escaped."

"You would go to such lengths to keep the villagers happy?" Tara said to Raka. "And let me guess, you chose Ananth for the job because there was something you could use to threaten him with, and so that I would never suspect him even if I did catch him loitering near our hut. That's why the *investigation* has not come up with anything, right?"

"I'm sorry, Tara," said Ananth. He looked as if he was about to cry. "You have no idea how much this has been eating me up inside."

"Because of what you did, our brother is dead!" shrieked Tara. She looked around at the villagers. "All of you are responsible for his death!"

Ananth's face was the colour of thin milk as he stared at Tara.

Yama put his hand on her shoulder. "Tara, I'm so very sorry."

Ananth stepped forward. "Tara, I'll do anything to make it up to you, I'll —"

"You've done quite enough," said Tara. She stepped forward and grasped Ananth's right hand. He stared at her, his eyes wide. "What …?"

Tara ripped the thin thread she had tied to his wrist ages ago, a symbol of the eternal bond between brother and sister, and threw it away. "A *real* brother would never have done what you did."

Ananth's stricken expression did not give her any satisfaction or relief.

"That wasn't the only thing, was it Ananth?" said Tara. "Something else compelled you to do this."

Ananth's voice broke. "I was jealous of you — of all the fame you've been getting. You always end up doing things on your own and surviving. It was a moment of madness when I agreed, Tara. Please forgive me. I was so very wrong."

Tara shook her head. These revelations weighed on her so heavily that for a moment she could think of nothing but the enormous betrayal by the very people she had loved and trusted.

"You won't have to be jealous of me ever again," said Tara. "I won't be staying long. Lord Yama is here to take me with him. It was one of the conditions of visiting the Underworld."

"What do you mean?" asked Raka. The other members of the Panchayat had gathered round him too.

"Tara sacrificed her life so that she could rid Morni of the real evil," replied Lord Yama. "But you cowards don't deserve this."

The shameful expressions on the villagers' faces should have given her joy, relief. But Tara felt empty. Layla had destroyed everything she had ever valued in her life. Suddenly she realized that Layla had slipped away yet again. "Layla's gone. Find her, don't let her get away!"

The crowd was galvanized into action. Everyone scattered. Tara was about to follow them. If Layla escaped, all this would have been in vain.

"Tara, it is time for us to go," said Lord Yama. "The villagers now know the truth and they'll deal with Layla."

Tara stared at him aghast. "My Lord, I need just a few more minutes. I want to have the satisfaction of doing what I set out to do — kill her. Please don't deny me that."

"Things do not work to your time, Tara. I have many other things that need my attention. We have spent far too long here."

Tara was about to plead once more when an agonized wail filled the air. It came from near the huts just beyond the clearing. Then there was silence. Tara pushed through the people who were already racing in the direction of the scream. Had Layla attacked someone else? Her mother? Almost faint with anxiety, she sprinted toward the scream.

She reached the shadows and found Layla. But she wasn't alone.

— twenty-eight —

Forgiveness

Someone brought a lantern that illuminated a scene Tara could never have imagined.

Gayatri stared calmly at the gathering crowd. The spotless white saree she normally wore was splotched with red. And Layla lay at her feet, the hilt of a kitchen knife protruding from her chest.

"What happened, Gayatri-ma?" said Tara in a trembling voice.

"You've carried this burden all by yourself for far too long," said Gayatri.

Tara walked up to them and dropped to her knees next to Layla, unable to believe that it had finally happened. Layla stared up at her with sightless eyes. Blood still oozed from the wound on her chest, the deep stain spreading on her kurta.

Tara waited for that feeling of elation to lift her up,

a bubble of joy to grow within her, relief to flood her. The only thing that she felt was a deep sadness for the dead child in front of her. Dead because of a misguided attempt at revenge by Layla's own mother. And Tara had been driven by the same desire: to avenge Suraj's death. She had always thought revenge would taste sweet, but it was not so. The bitter taste in her mouth was unbearable.

"Why?" asked Tara. She looked up at Gayatri, who was wiping her blood-stained hands on her saree. She looked serene.

"Why what, Tara?"

"Why did you do this? It was my job. That's why I came back."

"I know," said Gayatri. "I know more than you think I do."

The rest of the village, along with the Panchayat, arrived and gathered around them. Raka pushed his way to the front and stood beside them. "Oh my God, Gayatri," he said when he saw Layla. "What have you done?"

Both Tara and Gayatri ignored him.

"Know what, Gayatri-ma?" asked Tara. She looked closely at the smooth countenance that had always been tranquil, and a source of strength for her. Even now, there was not a flicker of fear on that face. How could the son of one so strong, turn out to be so weak?

"I know why you came back, Tara," said Gayatri. "I also know what my son foolishly agreed to do, to save me. He told me after the deed was done and that is why I was determined to keep you safe with me. If you can find it in your heart to forgive Ananth, I will be very grateful."

Tara glanced at Ananth, who had been standing there staring at his mother. He seemed to be in shock. She looked at Raka, who hadn't uttered a word. This would probably be the last straw for him. How would he and the villagers react to a widow killing a child even if it was Layla? Would they use this as an excuse to throw her out?

"I wish you hadn't, Gayatri-ma," said Tara. She was angry at herself for letting Layla slip away. And at the villagers for being so blind.

The familiar clip-clop of hooves broke the silence and Lord Yama rode up to them. "It is time to go."

Tara felt as if her feet had turned to lead. The realization that she would never see her family again crushed her. She hugged herself, trying hard not to sob in front of all the villagers. She wanted to beg Lord Yama for one more day, one more *hour*, so she could say goodbye to her mother. See Suraj's face one more time. But she knew it was futile. No matter how much time she had with them, it would never be enough. It was best to go now.

Tara sighed. "I'm ready," she said in unison with Gayatri.

'What are you talking about?" said Tara. She looked from Lord Yama to Gayatri, who had stepped forward.

"I'm the one going with Lord Yama," said Gayatri. "Not you, Tara. You still have a life to live."

"No!" yelled Ananth. "You can't leave me, Mother, I'll be an orphan."

Gayatri held out her arms and Ananth threw himself at her. "Listen to me," she said after a moment. "You have to let me go. I'll be a lot happier because I'll be with your father at last."

"I cannot let you do that, Gayatri-ma," said Tara. "Lord Yama, I was the one who came to the Underworld, I was the one who should have killed Layla. You can't take someone else in my stead."

"But you didn't, Tara. I killed Layla," said Gayatri. She stepped up to Lord Yama. "Lord, you know that taking me would be a kinder, wiser thing to do. For all of us."

Lord Yama looked at Gayatri, at Tara, then at the rest of the villagers. "These two members of Morni are the most hated, and are better than all of you put together," he said. He was quiet for a long moment. "All right, Gayatri. I will take you instead of Tara."

"No!" said Tara. "She did this for me. You said that once I came to the Underworld, I could not return to the land of the living."

"Tara, I make the rules, and I also have the power to make exceptions," said Yama. "You did not kill Layla, Gayatri did, so really, you have not completed what you set out to do."

Tara flung herself into Gayatri's arms. "Your son did so much to keep you alive and now you're going to leave him, leave me?"

"Tara, it's also because of his foolishness that I must go. This is to make up for what he did to you and your family. Will you please forgive Ananth, for my sake?"

Tara stepped back. "I don't know if I can."

Ananth hugged his mother tight, his face streaming with tears.

"You'll be fine, Ananth. Just remember everything I have ever taught you. No good comes from harming anyone, even if it is for a good cause."

Lord Yama turned the bull toward the forest. "Stay well, Tara. I hope that I never have to meet you again in your lifetime. Suraj's soul is already safe with me, but I will send someone for Layla." The bull started to move away and Gayatri followed.

Everyone watched her and Yama fade away into the dawn mist. Tara stood, listening to the sound of the hooves, until at last, it too died away.

Tara looked at the very dead Layla at her feet. Soon mother and daughter would be together in the Underworld and she couldn't help but feel a little relieved that she wouldn't have to face their wrath.

Tiredness pressed down on her with a giant fist, grinding her into the earth.

"You were willing to sacrifice your life for Morni," said Raka, "and we misjudged you. We let our beliefs and superstitions cloud our common sense. Can you ever forgive us, forgive me, Tara?"

"Me, too, Tara," said Ananth, very softly. "Please?"

Tara stared at all of them for a long moment. She really did not want to, but what would she achieve by carrying the hatred around in her heart? It would poison the rest of her life. Was it possible they could change?

A sliver of sun peeped over the horizon. Tara watched the glow spread across the sky, turning grey to gold, and knew that no matter what happened, there was one person whom she could always rely on — herself.

And that was all she really needed.

"I forgive you," she said.

— glossary —

Arre	Slang for "Oh."
Ayurvedic Medicine	Ayurveda is a system of traditional medicine, native to the Indian subcontinent and practised in other parts of the world as a form of alternative medicine.
Biryani	A South Asian dish made primarily of rice, spices, meat, and/or vegetables.
Blouse	Most commonly refers to a woman's shirt.
Coir	A coarse fibre extracted from the fibrous outer shell of a coconut.
Dupatta	A long, multi-purpose scarf that is essential to many South Asian women's suits.
Ganesh Temple	Place of worship for the elephant-headed god who is also considered

	the god of knowledge and the remover of obstacles.
Ghaghra-choli	A long, flowing skirt reaching the calves or ankles, worn with a fitted blouse with short sleeves.
Himalayas	A mountain range in Asia, separating the Indian subcontinent from the Tibetan Plateau.
Holi	Also called the Festival of Colours, celebrated by throwing coloured powder and coloured water at each other.
Kalyug	Or "Kali Yuga," is the last of the four stages that the world goes through as part of the cycle of yugas described in the Indian scriptures. The other ages are Satya Yuga, Treta Yuga, and Dvapara Yuga. Hindus believe that human civilization degenerates spiritually during the Kali Yuga, which is referred to as the Dark Age because in it, people are as far removed as possible from God.
Kurta-Pajama	A loose shirt falling just above or at the knees, and normally worn with loose trousers with a drawstring waistband.

Mantra	A mantra is a sound, syllable, word, or group of words that are considered capable of "creating transformation," normally of the spiritual kind.
Mojri	Also known as a "pagrakhi," is traditional ornamental leather footwear originating from Rajasthan.
Monsoon	A monsoon is traditionally defined as a seasonally reversing wind accompanied by seasonal changes in precipitation or heavy rain.
Pooja	A form of worship, that relates to dedication and belief in a particular god.
Poori	A South Asian unleavened bread commonly consumed in India, Pakistan, and Bangladesh. It is eaten for breakfast, as a snack or a light meal.
Prasad	Anything, usually edible, that is first offered to a deity and then distributed in His name. The prasad has the deity's blessing residing within it.
Raat-ki-Raani	A shrub that goes by the botanical name of *Cestrum Nocturnum*. Its light-green flowers open at night

	and emit an intoxicating fragrance.
Raita	An Indian condiment based on yogurt (dahi) and used as a sauce or dip. The yogurt is seasoned with coriander (cilantro), cumin, mint, cayenne pepper, and other herbs and spices.
Rakhi	Holy thread tied by a sister on her brother's wrist. The brother, in return, offers a gift to his sister and vows to protect her for as long as he lives.
Saree	Garment worn by females in the Indian subcontinent. A saree is a strip of unstitched cloth, ranging from four to nine metres in length, which is draped over the body in various styles.
Shalwar-Kameez	Is a traditional dress worn by both women and men in South Asia. Salwar or shalwar are loose pajama-like trousers. The kameez (shirt) is usually cut straight and flat. Women normally wear this with a dupatta.
Shendi	A long lock of hair gathered at the back of a normally bald head, resembling a pigtail.

Sindoor	A red powder (vermilion), which is traditionally applied at the beginning or completely along the part-line of a woman's hair (also called "mang") or as a dot on the forehead. Sindoor is the mark of a married woman in Hinduism.
Tandav	"Tāṇḍava" or "Tāṇḍava nṛtya," the divine art form, is a dance performed by the Hindu god, Shiva. According to Hindu mythology, Shiva's Tandava is a vigorous dance that is the source of the cycle of creation, preservation, and dissolution.
Thali	A round tray made of steel or silver with smaller bowls or compartments in which a variety of foods are served.
Turban	The word *turban* is a common umbrella term, loosely used in English to refer to several sorts of headwear.

— acknowledgements —

My heartfelt thanks to:

Rahul, Aftab, and Coby for putting up with me while I create my masterpiece. Mom, for always being there for me. Dad, who still continues to inspire me to do my best. The rest of my family in Toronto, Mumbai, and New Delhi, for your love and encouragement. Ayaan Indorewala, who brightens my day with his antics and adorable smile. Raunak and Simran Sood for your keen questions that make me think. Anne Lilly, Anne-Louise Gould, and Lies Weijs for your warmth and friendship. And finally, thank you to my wonderful editor, Shannon Whibbs, and the Dundurn team for continuing to believe in Tara and in me.